ERLE STANLEY GARDNER

- Cited by the Guinness Book of World Records as the #1 bestselling writer of all time!

- Author of more than 130 clever, authentic, and sophisticated mystery novels!

- Creator of the amazing Perry Mason, the savvy Della Street, and dynamite detective Paul Drake!

- THE ONLY AUTHOR WHO OUT-SELLS AGATHA CHRISTIE, HAROLD ROBBINS, BARBARA CARTLAND, AND LOUIS L'AMOUR *COMBINED!*

Why?

Because he writes the best, most fascinating whodunits of all!

You'll want to read every one of them, coming soon from
BALLANTINE BOOKS

Also by Erle Stanley Gardner
Published by Ballantine Books:

THE CASE OF THE BEAUTIFUL BEGGAR

THE CASE OF THE LAZY LOVER

THE CASE OF THE FIERY FINGER

THE CASE OF THE SHAPELY SHADOW

THE CASE OF THE HAUNTED HUSBAND

THE CASE OF THE GRINNING GORILLA

THE CASE OF THE VAGABOND VIRGIN

THE CASE OF THE RESTLESS REDHEAD

The Case of the
Perjured Parrot

Erle Stanley Gardner

BALLANTINE BOOKS • NEW YORK

ISBN 0-345-30396-2

This edition published by arrangement with
William Morrow and Company, Inc.

Manufactured in the United States of America

First Ballantine Books Edition: June 1982

CAST OF CHARACTERS

PERRY MASON—Noted criminal lawyer—intrepid, dramatic, elusive fighter, whose cause is never lost 1

DELLA STREET—His secretary, whose horizon is bounded by that of her chief, and whose only fear is that some day he may overstep the charmed circle of his daring 1

CHARLES SABIN—Son of Fremont C. Sabin, a substantial citizen, quiet, determined, ready to pay anything to bring his father's murderer to justice 7

PAUL DRAKE—Detective, long, laconic, and loyal, willing to toss his natural caution to the winds in the service of Perry Mason 13

SERGEANT HOLCOMB—One-track representative of the long arm of the law, with a wistful, pugnacious hope of catching Perry Mason off his guard 17

SHERIFF BARNES—Efficient, tolerant, slow, who would rather be sure of his man 17

RICHARD WAID—Erstwhile secretary to Fremont C. Sabin, whose conscience is his guide, when convenient 26

ARTHUR GIBBS—Calmly observant trainer of parrots to suit the public taste 35

Mrs. WINTERS—Neighbor of Helen Monteith, whose friendship isn't quite deep enough to drown her curiosity 42

HELEN MONTEITH—Buffeted by the winds of circumstance, whose ship finally reaches port 47

Mrs. HELEN WATKINS SABIN—Widow of the murdered man—a juggernaut with a purpose 59

STEVE WATKINS—Suave son of Mrs. Watkins by a former marriage, and her able disciple 59

DISTRICT ATTORNEY RAYMOND SPRAGUE—Explosive, frustrated exponent of the high-pressure technique 71

RANDOLPH BOLDING—Handwriting expert, who found to his surprise that professional pride had better be denied 108

ANDY TEMPLET—Practical, non-partisan coroner, determined that justice shall be done 127

GEORGE WALLMAN—Innocent bystander, whose simple philosophy is the cause of much confusion 164

CHAPTER ONE

PERRY MASON regarded the pasteboard jacket, labeled "IMPORTANT UNANSWERED CORRESPONDENCE," with uncordial eyes.

Della Street, his secretary, looking as crisply efficient as a nurse in a freshly starched uniform, said with her best Monday-morning air, "I've gone over it carefully, Chief. The letters on top are the ones you simply *have* to answer. I've cleaned out a whole bunch of the correspondence from the bottom."

"From the bottom?" Mason asked. "How did you do that?"

"Well," she confessed, "it's stuff that's been in there too long."

Mason tilted back in his swivel chair, crossed his long legs, assumed his best lawyer manner and said, in mock cross-examination, "Now, let's get this straight, Miss Street. Those were letters which had originally been put in the 'IMPORTANT UNANSWERED' file?"

"Yes."

"And you've gone over that file from time to time, carefully?"

"Yes."

"And eliminated everything which didn't require my personal attention?"

"Yes."

"And yet this morning of Monday, September twelfth, you take out a large number of letters from the bottom of the file?"

"That's right," she admitted, her eyes twinkling.

"How many letters, may I ask?"

"Oh, fifteen or twenty."

"And did you answer those yourself?"

She shook her head, smiling.

"What *did* you do with them?" Mason asked.

"Transferred them to another file."

"What file?"

"The 'LAPSED' file."

Mason chuckled delightedly. "Now *there's* an idea, Della. We simply hold things in the 'IMPORTANT UNANSWERED' file until a lapse of time robs them of their importance, and then we transfer them to the 'LAPSED' file. It eliminates correspondence, saves worry, and gets me away from office routine, which I detest. . . . Incidentally, Della, things which seem frightfully important at the time have a habit of fading into insignificance. Events are like telephone poles, streaming back past the observation platform of a speeding train. They loom large at first, then melt into the distance, becoming so tiny they finally disappear altogether. . . . That's the way with nearly all of the things we think are so vital."

Her eyes were wide and innocent. "Do the telephone poles *really* get smaller, Chief, or do they just appear smaller?"

"Of course, they don't *get* smaller," he said; "it's simply that you're farther away from them. Other telephone poles come in and fill up the foreground. The telephone poles are all the same size. However, as you get farther distant from them they appear to be smaller, and . . ." He broke off abruptly and said, "Wait a minute. You aren't gently trying to point out a fallacy in my argument, are you?"

At her triumphant grin, he made a mock grimace. "I should have known better than to argue with a woman. All right, Simon Legree, get your notebook ready, and we'll write those confounded letters."

He opened the filing jacket, scanned a letter from a prominent firm of lawyers, tossed it across the desk to her, and said, "Write these people that I'm not interested in handling the case, even at twice the fee named. It's just a plain, ordinary murder case. A woman gets tired of her husband, plugs him with a six-gun, and then weeps and wails that he was drunk and trying to beat her up. She lived with him for six years, and seeing him drunk was no novelty. The business about being afraid he was going to kill her doesn't check with the story of the other witnesses."

2

"How much of that," Della Street asked with calm efficiency, "do you want me to put in the letter?"

"Just the part about not wanting to handle the case. . . . Oh, Lord, here's another one. A man, who's swindled a bunch of people into buying worthless stock, wants me to prove that he was within the letter of the law."

Mason slammed the file shut and said, "You know, Della, I wish people would learn to differentiate between the reputable lawyer who represents persons accused of crime, and the criminal lawyer who becomes a silent partner in the profits of crime."

"Just how would you explain the difference?" she asked.

Mason said, "Crime is personal. Evidence of crime is impersonal. I never take a case unless I'm convinced my client was incapable of committing the crime charged. Once I've reached that conclusion, I figure there must be some discrepancy between the evidence and the conclusions the police have drawn from that evidence. I set out to find them."

She laughed. "You sound as though you were more of a detective than a lawyer."

"No," Mason said, "they are two different professions. A detective gathers evidence. He becomes skilled in knowing what to look for, where to find it, and how to get it. A lawyer interprets the evidence after it's been collected. He gradually learns . . ."

He was interrupted by the ringing of the telephone at Della's desk. She answered it, saying, "Hold the line a moment, please," and then, cupping her hand over the mouthpiece, turned to Perry Mason. "Would you be interested in seeing a Mr. Charles Sabin on a matter of the greatest importance? Mr. Sabin says he's willing to pay any consultation fee."

Mason said, "Depends on what he wants. If he has a murder case, I'll listen to him. If he wants me to draw up a chattel mortgage, the answer is 'no.' There isn't enough money in the mint to tempt me to . . . Wait a minute, Della. What's his name?"

"Sabin," she said, "Charles W. Sabin."

"Where is he?"

"In the outer office."

Mason said, "Tell him to wait a few minutes. No, wait a minute. Find out if he's related to Fremont C. Sabin."

Della asked the question over the telephone, and waited for the girl at the information desk in the outer office to relay the inquiry to the visitor. She turned once more to Mason and said, "Yes, he's the son of Mr. Fremont C. Sabin."

"Tell him I'll see him," Mason said. "Tell him he'll have to wait about ten minutes. Go out and meet him, Della. Size him up. Take him into the law library, let him wait there. Bring me the morning newspapers. This, young lady, in case you don't know it, is a Break with a capital 'B.' Okay, get busy . . . Wait a minute, I have one of the newspapers here."

Mason made a dive for the newspaper, sweeping the file of important correspondence over to the far end of the desk, as he hurriedly cleared a space in front of him.

The account of the murder of Fremont C. Sabin occupied much of the front page. There were photographs on the second and third pages. There was a human interest story about his character and personality.

That which was known of the murder was well calculated to stir the imagination. Fremont C. Sabin, eccentric multimillionaire, had virtually retired from the many businesses which bore his name. His son, Charles Sabin, carried on for him. During the past two years the wealthy man had become almost a recluse. At times he would travel in a trailer, stopping in at auto camps, fraternizing with other trailerites, talking politics, exchanging views. None of those with whom he talked had the least inkling that this man, with his shiny business suit, his diffident manner, and his quiet gray eyes, was rated at more than two million dollars.

Or he would disappear for a week or two at a time, prowling around through bookstores, dropping in at libraries, living in a realm of studious abstraction, while he browsed through books.

Librarians invariably classified him as a clerk out of work.

Of late he had been spending much of his time in a

4

mountain cabin, on the pine-clad slope of a rugged range near a brawling stream. Here he would sit on the porch by the hour with a pair of powerful binoculars in his hand, watching the birds, making friends with the chipmunks and squirrels, reading books—asking only to be let alone.

Just touching sixty, he represented a strange figure of a man; one who had wrung from life all that it offered in the way of material success; a man who literally had more money than he knew what to do with. Some of this money he had established in trust funds, but for the most part he did not believe in philanthropy, thinking that the ultimate purpose of life was to develop character; that the more a person came to depend on outside assistance, the more his character was weakened.

The newspaper published an interview with Charles Sabin, the son of the murdered man, giving an insight into his father's character. Mason read it with interest. Sabin had believed that life was a struggle and had purposely been made a struggle; that competition developed character; that victory was of value only as it marked the goal of achievement; that to help someone else toward victory was doing that person an injustice, since victories were progressive.

The elder Sabin had placed something over a million dollars in trust funds for charitable uses, but he had stipulated that the money was to go only to those who had been incapacitated in life's battles: the crippled, the aged, the infirm. To those who could still struggle on, Sabin offered nothing. The privilege of struggling for achievement was the privilege of living, and to take away that right to struggle was equivalent to taking away life itself.

Della Street entered Mason's office as he finished reading that portion of the article.

"Well?" Mason asked.

"He's interesting," she said. "Of course he's taking it pretty hard. It's something of a shock, but there's nothing hysterical about him, and nothing affected about his grief. He's quiet, determined, and very self-controlled."

"How old?" Mason asked.

"About thirty-two or thirty-three. Quietly dressed . . . In fact, that's the impression he gives you, of being quiet. His voice is low and well-modulated. His eyes are a very cold blue, and very, very steady, if you get what I mean."

"I think I do," Mason told her. "Rather spare and austere in his appearance?"

"Yes, with high cheekbones and a firm mouth. I think you'll find he does a lot of thinking. He's that type."

Mason said, "All right, let's get some more facts on this murder."

He once more devoted his attention to reading the newspaper, then abruptly said, "There's too much hooey mixed in with this, Della, to give us very much information. I suppose I should get the highlights, because he probably won't want to talk about it."

He returned to the newspaper, skimming salient facts from the account of the murder.

Fishing season in the Grizzly Creek had opened on Tuesday, September sixth. It had been closed until that date by order of the Fish and Game Commission to protect the late season fishing. Fremont C. Sabin had gone to his mountain cabin, ready to take advantage of the first day. Police reconstructed what had happened at that cabin from the circumstantial evidence which remained. He had evidently retired early, setting the alarm for five-thirty in the morning. He had arisen, cooked breakfast, donned his fishing things, and had returned about noon, evidently with a limit of fish. Sometime after that—and the police, from the evidence which had been so far made available, were unable to tell just when—Fremont Sabin had been murdered. Robbery had evidently not been the motive, since a well-filled wallet was found in his pocket. He was still wearing a diamond ring, and a valuable emerald stickpin was found in the drawer of the dresser, near the bed. He had been shot through the heart and at close range by a short-barreled derringer, obsolete in design but deadly in its efficiency.

Sabin's pet parrot, who had of late years accompanied him on nearly all his trips to the mountain cabin, had been left in the room with the body. The murderer had fled.

The mountain cabin was isolated, nearly a hundred yards back from the automobile road which wound its tortuous way up to the pine-timbered cabin. There was not a great deal of traffic on this road, and those people who lived in the neighborhood had learned to leave the wealthy recluse alone.

Day after day such traffic as used the highway passed heedlessly by, while in the cabin back under the trees a screaming parrot kept vigil over the lifeless corpse of his master.

Not until several days after the murder, on Sunday, September eleventh, when fishermen came in large numbers to line the stream, did anyone suspect anything was wrong.

By that time the parrot's shrill, raucous cries, interspersed with harsh profanity, attracted attention.

"Polly wants something to eat. Dammit, Polly wants something to eat. Don't you damn fools know Polly's hungry?"

A neighbor, who owned a nearby cabin, had investigated. Peering through the windows he had seen the parrot, and then had seen something else which made him telephone for the police.

The murderer had evidently had compassion for the bird, but none for the master. The cage door had been left propped open. Someone, apparently the murderer, had left a dish of water on the floor, an abundance of food near the cage. Food remained, but the water dish was dry.

Mason looked up from the newspaper and said to Della Street, "All right, Della, let's have him in."

Charles Sabin shook hands with Perry Mason, glanced at the newspaper on the table, and said, "I hope you are familiar with the facts surrounding my father's death."

Mason nodded, waited until his visitor had seated himself in the overstuffed, black leather chair, and then inquired, "Just what do you want me to do?"

"Quite a few things," Sabin said. "Among others, I want you to see that my father's widow, Helen Watkins

7

Sabin, doesn't ruin the business. I have reason to believe there's a will leaving the bulk of the estate to me, and, in particular, making me the executor. I can't find that will in searching among his papers. I'm afraid it may be in her possession. She's fully capable of destroying it. I don't want her to act as administratrix of the estate."

"You dislike her?"

"Very much."

"Your father was a widower?"

"Yes."

"When did he marry his present wife?"

"About two years ago."

"Are there any other children?"

"No. His widow has a grown son, however."

"Was this last marriage a success? Was your father happy?"

"No. He was *very* unhappy. He realized he'd been victimized. He would have asked for an annulment, or a divorce, if it hadn't been for his dread of publicity."

"Go on," Mason said. "Tell me just what you want me to do."

"I'm going to put my cards on the table," Charles Sabin told him. "My legal affairs are handled by Cutter, Grayson & Bright. I want you to co-operate with them."

"You mean in the probate of the estate?" Mason asked.

Sabin shook his head. "My father was murdered. I want you to co-operate with the police in bringing that murderer to justice.

"My father's widow is going to require quite a bit of handling. I think it's a job that's beyond the abilities of Cutter, Grayson & Bright. I want you to handle it.

"I am, of course, deeply shocked by what has happened. I was notified yesterday afternoon by the police. It's been very much of an ordeal. I can assure you that no ordinary business matter would have brought me out today."

Mason looked at the lines of suffering etched on the man's face, and said, "I can readily understand that."

"And," Sabin went on, "I realize there are certain

questions you'll want to ask. I'd like to make the interview as brief as possible."

Mason said, "I'll need some sort of authorization to . . ."

Sabin took a wallet from his pocket. "I think I have anticipated your reasonable requirements, Mr. Mason. Here is a retainer check, together with a letter stating that you are acting as my lawyer and are to have access to any and all of the property left by my father."

Mason took the letter and check. "I see," he said, "that you are a methodical man."

"I try to be," Sabin told him. "The check will be in the nature of a retainer. Do you consider it adequate?"

"It's more than adequate," Mason said, smiling. "It's generous."

Sabin inclined his head. "I've followed your career with a great deal of interest, Mr. Mason. I think you have exceptional legal ability and an uncanny deductive skill. I want to avail myself of both."

"Thanks," the lawyer said. "If I'm going to be of any value to you, Mr. Sabin, I'll want an absolutely free hand."

"In what respect?" Sabin asked.

"I want to be free to do just as I please in the matter. If the police should charge someone with the crime, I want the privilege of representing that person. In other words, I want to clear up the crime in my own way."

"Why do you ask that?" Sabin said. "Surely I'm paying you enough . . ."

"It isn't that," Mason told him, "but if you've followed my cases, you'll note that most of them have been cleared up in the courtroom. I can suspect the guilty, but about the only way I can really prove my point is by cross-examining witnesses."

"I see your point," Sabin conceded. "I think it's entirely reasonable."

"And," Mason said, "I'll want to know all of the salient facts, everything which you can give me that will be of assistance."

Sabin settled back in the chair. He spoke calmly, almost disinterestedly. "There are two or three things to be taken into consideration in getting a perspective on my father's life. One of them was the fact that he and my mother were very happily married. My mother was a wonderful woman. She had a loyalty which was unsurpassed, and a complete lack of nervousness. During all her married life, there was literally never an unkind word spoken, simply because she never allowed herself to develop any of those emotional reflexes, which so frequently make people want to bicker with those whom they love, or with whom they come in constant association.

Naturally, my father came to judge every woman by *her* standards. After her death, he was exceedingly lonely. His present wife was employed in the capacity of housekeeper. She was shrewd, scheming, deadly, designing, avaricious, grasping. She set about to insinuate herself into his affections. She did so deliberately. My father had never had any experience with women of her kind. He was temperamentally unfitted to deal with her in the first place, or even to comprehend her character. As a result, he permitted himself to be hypnotized into marriage. He has, of course, been desperately unhappy."

"Where is Mrs. Sabin now?" Mason asked. "I believe the paper mentioned something about her being on a tour."

"Yes, she left on a round-the-world cruise about two and a half months ago. She was located by wireless on a ship which left the Panama Canal yesterday. A plane has been chartered to meet her at one of the Central American ports, and she should arrive here tomorrow morning."

"And she will try to take charge?" Mason asked.

"Very completely," Sabin said, in a voice which spoke volumes.

"Of course, as a son," Mason said, "you have certain rights."

Sabin said wearily, "One of the reasons that I have set aside my grief in order to come to you at this time, Mr. Mason, is that whatever you do should be well started before she arrives. She is a very competent woman, and a very ruthless adversary."

"I see," Mason said.

"She has a son by a former marriage, Steven Watkins,"

Sabin went on. "I have sometimes referred to him as his mother's stool pigeon. He has developed conscious affability as an asset. He has the technique of a politician, the character of a rattl snake. He has been East for some time, and took the plane from New York to connect with the plane that will pick up his mother in Central America. They will arrive together."

"How old is he?" Mason asked.

"Twenty-six. His mother managed to put him through college. He looks on an education only as a magic formula, which should enable him to go through life without work. As a young man he advocated a share-the-wealth philosophy as something which would reward him for living without making it necessary for him to engage in competitive work. After his mother married my father, she was able to wheedle him into giving her large sums of money which were squandered upon Steve with a lavish hand. He has reacted just as one would expect him to under the circumstances. He is now extremely contemptuous of what he refers to as the 'common herd.'"

"Have *you*," Mason asked, "any idea of who murdered your father?"

"None whatever. If I did have, I would try to dismiss it from my mind. I don't want to even think of anyone whom I know in that connection until I have proof. And when I have proof, Mr. Mason, I want the law to take its course."

"Did your father have any enemies?"

"No. Except . . . there are two things which I think you should know about, Mr. Mason. One of them, the police know, the other, they don't."

"What are they?" Mason asked.

"It was not mentioned in the newspapers," Sabin said, "but in the cabin were certain intimate articles of feminine wearing apparel. *I* think those clothes were left there by the murderer, simply to swing public sympathy toward the widow."

"What else?" Mason asked. "You mentioned something which the police didn't know about. Was that . . ."

Sabin said, "This is something which may be significant, Mr. Mason. I believe you have read in the newspapers of my father's attachment for his parrot."

Mason nodded.

"Casanova was a present given to my father by his brother three or four years ago. His brother's a great parrot fancier, and Dad became very much attached to the bird. It was with him frequently . . . And the parrot which was found in the cabin with my father's body, and which the police and everyone else have assumed to be Casanova, is, in fact, *not my father's parrot*."

Mason's eyes showed keen interest. "You're certain?" he asked.

"Absolutely certain."

"May I ask how you know?"

"In the first place," Sabin said, "the parrot in the cabin is given to profanity, particularly in connection with requests for food. Casanova had never learned to swear."

"Perhaps," Mason said, "a change of environment would have been responsible for that. You know, a parrot can pick up . . ."

"Moreover," Sabin said, "—and you'll pardon me if I interrupt you, Mr. Mason, because I am about to mention a point which is irrefutable—Casanova had one claw missing, a claw on his right foot. This parrot does not."

Mason frowned. "But why the devil," he asked, "should anyone want to substitute parrots?"

"The only reason I can think of," Sabin said, "is that the parrot is more important than would at first seem to be the case. I am quite certain that Casanova was with my father in the mountain cabin when my father was murdered. He, perhaps, saw something, or heard something, so he was removed and another parrot substituted. My father returned home on Friday, September second, long enough to pick up Casanova. We hadn't expected him until Monday, September fifth."

"But it would have been so much simpler and easier for the murderer to have killed the parrot," Mason said.

"I realize that," Sabin replied, "and I know that my theory is bizarre. Nevertheless, it is the only explanation I have been able to make in my own mind."

"Why," Mason asked, "didn't you tell the police about this?"

Sabin shook his head. This time there was no attempt to disguise the weariness in his eyes or his voice. "I have come to realize," he said, "that it is absolutely impossible for the police to keep matters from the newspapers, and I don't have any great confidence in the ability of the police to solve a crime such as this. I think you will find that it has very deep ramifications, Mr. Mason. I've told the police no more than was absolutely necessary. I have not volunteered information. I am giving this information to you. I would suggest that you keep it from the police. Let them build up their own case."

And Sabin indicated that he had told everything he knew by getting to his feet and extending his hand. "Thank you very much, Mr. Mason," he said. "I'll rest a lot easier in knowing that the matter is in your hands."

CHAPTER TWO

MASON, pacing back and forth across his office, jerked out comments. Paul Drake, head of the Drake Detective Agency, his tall form draped crosswise across the over-stuffed leather chair, made notes in a leather-backed notebook.

"That substituted parrot," Mason said, "is a clue which we have in advance of the police. . . . It's a profane parrot. . . . Later on, we're going to find out why the murderer wanted to substitute parrots. Right now, we're going to try and trace the profane parrot, which should be easy. . . . We can't hope to compete with the police, so we'll ignore the commonplace factors."

"How about the pink silk nightie?" Paul Drake asked, in his slow, drawling voice. "Do we do anything about that?"

"Not a thing," Mason said. "That's something the police are working on tooth and nail. . . . How much do you know about the case, Paul?"

"Not very much more than what I've read in the papers," Drake said, "but one of my friends, who's in the newspaper game, was asking me something about weapons."

"What did he want to know?" Mason asked.

"Something about the murder gun."

"What about the gun?"

"It's some sort of a trick weapon," Drake said. "One of those short-barreled guns, with a trigger which folds back out of the way. It's small enough to be carried anywhere."

"What caliber?"

"A forty-one."

"Try and find out about ammunition for it," Mason said. "See if the shells are carried in stock . . . No, forget it. The police will do all that. You stick to parrots, Paul. Cover all pet stores. Find out about parrot sales during the last week or two."

Paul Drake, whose efficiency as a detective depended in large part upon the fact that he looked so completely innocuous, closed his leather-backed notebook and dropped it into his pocket. He surveyed Perry Mason with slightly protruding eyes, the expression of which was habitually masked by a glassy film.

"How far do you want me to check up on Mrs. Sabin and the son, Perry?" he asked.

"Everything you can find out," Mason said.

Drake checked off the points on his fingers. "Let's see now, if I have everything straight. Get the dope on the widow and Steve Watkins. Cover the bird stores and find out about the profane parrot. Get all the information I can about the mountain cabin and what happened up there. Get photographs of the interior, and . . . How about the exterior, Perry, do you want them?"

"No," Mason said, "I'm going to drive up there, Paul, and give it the once-over. The only photographs I want are those which were taken when the police discovered the body."

"On my way," Drake told him, sliding out of the chair.

"And incidentally," Mason said, as the detective was

halfway to the door, "here's another hunch. Let's suppose the murderer substituted parrots, then what became of Casanova?"

"I'll bite," Drake said, with a grin, "what do you do with a parrot? Make a parrot pie, or do you broil 'em on toast?"

Mason said, "You put them in cages and listen to them talk."

"No, really!" Drake exclaimed in mock surprise. "You don't tell me."

Mason said, "Get it through that droopy mind of yours that I'm not joking. That's *exactly* what you do with a parrot, and whoever took Casanova, may have done it because he wanted to listen to something Casanova had to say."

"That," Drake admitted, "is a thought."

"Moreover," Mason went on, "the murderer probably has moved into a new neighborhood. You might make a check on any new parrots."

"What do you want me to do?" Drake asked. "Take a bird census, or put a bird bath on the roof and watch for parrots . . . My God, Perry, have a heart! How the devil can a man find a new parrot?"

"I think," Mason told him, "you'll find there aren't so many parrots. They're a noisy pet, and they aren't particularly apartment pets. People who have parrots are apt to live in the suburbs. Parrots are something of a nuisance as far as neighbors are concerned. I think there's a city ordinance on parrots in apartments. I have an idea you may find something from talking to pet stores. Trace the sale of new cages. Find out people who have been inquiring about the care and feeding of parrots. And incidentally, Paul, remember there's a pet store here in the block. Karl Helmold, the chap who runs it, is a client of mine. He'll probably have some trade lists, which will give you the names of the larger pet stores in the vicinity, and he may be able to tell you quite a bit about parrots. Put every available operative on the job."

"Okay," Drake said. "I'll be on my way."

Mason nodded to Della Street. "Come on, Della, let's go take a look at that cabin."

The road wound up the sides of the long canyon, turning and twisting on itself like a snake in pain. Through the windshield Mason caught occasional glimpses of purple mountains. Below, a threadlike stream tumbled whitely over granite boulders. Back of the car the heat haze of the valley country showed as a gaseous blanket, heavy, oppressive, shimmering.

It was dry up here, and the air was impregnated with scent which oozed from the tips of pine needles. It was hot, too, but the dry balsam-laden heat was kind to the nostrils. High overhead the southern California sky was so blue that it almost seemed black in contrast with the bright sunlight which beat down upon the sheer granite ridges where there was not enough soil to support trees.

They came to a shaded turn in the road, where a spring trickled into a natural basin, then overflowed, to spill through a culvert into a stream which plunged into the dark obscurity of tangled greenery.

Mason stopped the car and said, "We'll let the motor cool, and have a drink of mountain water. . . . Hello, here comes a police car."

He pointed down the side of the mountain to where a section of the road showed almost directly below them. A car, winding its laborious way up the long ascent, showed glinting red from a police spotlight fastened on the upper right-hand corner of the windshield.

"Do we try to beat them up?" Della Street asked.

Mason, stretching his long legs, sucked in deep breaths of the dry mountain air, and said, "No. We'll wait and follow. It will save time locating the cabin."

They drank the cool water, bending over the rock basin to place pursed lips against the limpid surface of the little pool. Gradually, above the sound of the wind sighing through the eloquent pines, came the grinding of a motor, whining in gear as it labored up the steep ascent.

As the car came into sight around the turn, Mason said, "I believe it's our old friend, Sergeant Holcomb, from headquarters. . . . Now, why should *he* be interested in a murder case which took place outside of the city . . . He's stopping."

The car veered abruptly from the paved highway to

come to a stop on the shaded parking space at the side of the road. A big man, who wore a broad-brimmed black Stetson, was the first to emerge. He was followed, a moment later, by Sergeant Holcomb of the Metropolitan Police.

Holcomb walked truculently across to Mason. "What the devil are *you* doing *here?*" he asked.

Mason said, "Odd, Sergeant, but I was thinking the same about you."

Sergeant Holcomb said, "I'm helping out Sheriff Barnes. He telephoned in for assistance, and the police loaned me to him. Shake hands with Perry Mason, Sheriff."

The sheriff, a big man in the late fifties, who moved with slow efficiency, swung out a bronzed hand which engulfed Mason's fingers. Mason introduced Della Street, and then produced the letter which Charles Sabin had given him. The Sheriff was impressed.

Sergeant Holcomb glanced from the letter to Mason. There was suspicion in his eyes, as well as in his voice. "Sabin employed you?"

"Yes."

"And gave you this letter?"

"Yes."

"Just what does he want you to do?"

"He wants me to co-operate with the police."

Sergeant Holcomb's laugh was sarcastic. "That's the best one I've heard in twenty years. Perry Mason co-operating with the police! You co-operate with the police just like the Republicans co-operate with the Democrats."

Mason turned to the sheriff. "Just because a lawyer represents innocent defendants doesn't mean he's opposed to the authorities," he said quietly.

"The hell it doesn't!" Sergeant Holcomb interpolated. "You've always been against the police."

"On the contrary," Mason told him, "I've helped solve quite a few murder cases."

"You've always managed to get *your* clients acquitted," Sergeant Holcomb pointed out.

"Exactly," Mason said. "It happened that the police were trying to convict innocent parties. It remained for

17

me to prove my clients innocent by finding the real murderers."

Sergeant Holcomb flushed, stepped forward, and started to say something, but Sheriff Barnes interposed what was apparently an unintentional shoulder. "Now listen, boys," he said, "there's nothing to argue about. I'm the sheriff of this county. This thing is just a little bit high-powered for me. I ain't got the facilities to make an investigation on this the way I'd like to, and I asked the city police to loan me a man who could help out with fingerprint work, and give me some suggestions. As far as I'm concerned, I'm going to be glad of any assistance I can get, and I don't care who gives it. I've read about some of Mason's cases in the newspapers. To my mind, when a lawyer proves his client innocent of crime by showing that someone else is guilty, he's done society a darn good turn, and the police have no kick coming."

"Well," Sergeant Holcomb said to the sheriff, "it's *your* funeral. His methods are enough to give you gray hairs."

Sheriff Barnes tilted back the sombrero and ran his fingers through sweat-moistened hair. "I've got gray hairs now," he said. "How about it, Mason, you going up?"

"I'll follow you," Mason told him. "You know the way?"

"Sure, I was up there nearly all day yesterday."

"How much has been touched?" Mason asked.

"Not a thing. We've taken the body out, and cleaned out the remains of a string of fish, which had gone pretty bad. Of course, we took the parrot. Aside from that, we ain't touched a thing, except to go over everything for fingerprints."

"Find any?" Mason asked.

"Quite a few," the sheriff admitted noncommittally.

Sergeant Holcomb said abruptly, "Well, Sheriff, let's get going. Mason can follow us."

The road crossed a ridge, debouched onto a plateau. Here and there were little clearings, cabins nestled back against the trees. Up near the upper end of the plateau, when they were within a few hundred feet of the stream which came roaring down from a mountain canyon,

18

Sheriff Barnes abruptly signaled for a right-hand turn. He swung into a dirt road, carpeted with pine needles, which ran back to a cabin so skillfully blended with the trees that it seemed almost to be the work of nature rather than of man.

Mason exclaimed, "Look at that cabin, Della! It certainly is a beautiful setting!"

A bluejay, resenting their intrusion, launched himself downward from the top of one of the pine trees, screeching his raucous, *"Thief . . . thief . . . thief."*

Mason swung the car into the shaded area back of the cabin and parked it. Sheriff Barnes crossed over and said, "I'm going to ask you to be careful not to touch anything, Mr. Mason, and I think Miss Street had better wait outside."

Mason nodded acquiescence.

A tall, rangy man who moved with the easy grace of a mountain dweller emerged from the shadows and touched his somewhat battered hat to the sheriff. "Everything's okay, Sheriff," he said.

Sheriff Barnes took a key from his pocket, unlocked the padlock on the door, and said by way of introduction, "This is Fred Waner. He lives up here. I've had him guarding the cabin."

The sheriff opened the door. "Now, let's try not to walk around any more than is necessary. You, Sergeant, know what to do." Mason glanced into the mountain cabin with its big fireplace, plain pine table, hand-hewn rafters. A neatly made bed with snowy linen was in startling contrast to the seed-littered floor. Mud-stained rubber boots stood, sagging limply; above them was a jointed fly rod.

Sergeant Holcomb said, "My advice, Sheriff, would be to let Mr. Mason look around without touching anything, and then leave. *We* can't do anything as long as he's here."

"Why not?" Sheriff Barnes said.

Sergeant Holcomb flushed. "For various reasons. One of them is that before you get done, this man is going to be on the other side of the fence. He's going to be opposing you, he's going to be trying to tear down the case you're building up against the murderer. The more you expose your methods to him, the more he has an opportunity to tear you to pieces on the witness stand."

Sheriff Barnes said doggedly, "That's all right. If anybody's going to be hung for murder on my say-so, I want it to be after a case is built up which can't be torn down."

"I'd like to see as much as you care to show me," Mason said to the sheriff. "I take it, that chalk outline on the floor represents where the body was found when it was first discovered."

"Yes, that's right. The gun was found over there about ten feet away, where you'll notice the outline in chalk."

"Is it possible that Mr. Sabin could have shot himself?" Mason asked.

"Absolutely impossible according to the testimony of the doctors. What's more, the gun had been wiped free of fingerprints. Sabin wasn't wearing gloves. If he'd shot himself, he'd have left some fingerprints on the gun."

Mason, frowning thoughtfully, said, "Then the murderer didn't even want it to look like suicide."

"How so?" the sheriff asked.

"He could very easily have placed the gun nearer the body. He could have wiped off his own fingerprints, and pressed the weapon into the hand of the dead man."

"That's logical," the sheriff said.

"And," Mason went on, "the murderer must have wanted the officers to find the gun."

"Baloney," Sergeant Holcomb said. "The murderer simply didn't want the officers to find the gun *on him*. That's the way all clever murderers do. As soon as they commit a crime, they drop the rod. They don't even keep it with them long enough to find some place to hide it. The gun can hang them. They shoot it and drop it."

"All right," Mason said, smiling, "you win. They shoot it and drop it. What else, Sheriff?"

"The parrot cage was over here on the floor," the sheriff said, "and the door was propped open with a little stick so the parrot could walk out whenever he wanted to."

"Or walk in, whenever it had been out?" Mason asked.

"Well, yes. That's a thought."

"And how long do you think the parrot had been here without food or water, Sheriff?"

"He'd had plenty of food. The water had dried up in the pan. See that agateware pan over there? Well, that had evidently been left pretty well filled with water, but the water had dried out—what the parrot hadn't had to drink. You can see little spots of rust on the bottom which show where the last few drops evaporated."

"The body then," Mason said, "must have been here for some time before it was discovered."

"The murder," Sheriff Barnes asserted, "took place some time on Tuesday, the sixth of September. It took place probably right around eleven o'clock in the morning."

"How do you figure that?" Mason asked. "Or do you object to telling me?"

"Not at all," the sheriff said. "The fishing season in this entire district opened on September sixth. The Fish and Game Commission wanted to have an area for fall fishing which hadn't been all fished out. So they picked out certain streams which they kept closed until later on in the season. This was one of the last. The season opened here on September sixth.

"Now then, Sabin was a funny chap. He had places that he went and things that he did, and we haven't found out all of 'em yet. We know some of them. He had a trailer and he'd drive around at trailer camps, sit and whittle and talk with people, just finding out that way what was going on in the world. Sometimes he'd take an old suit of shiny clothes and go prowl around libraries for a week or two . . ."

"Yes, I read all about that in the newspaper," Mason interrupted.

"Well," the sheriff went on, "he told his son and Richard Waid, his secretary, that he was going to be home on Monday the fifth to pick up his fishing things. He'd been away on a little trip. They don't know just where, but he surprised them by coming home on Friday the second. He took his fishing tackle, picked up his parrot, and came up here. It seems he was putting across a big deal in New

York, and had told his secretary to charter a plane and be ready to fly East when he gave the word. The secretary waited at the airport all Monday afternoon. He had a plane in readiness. About ten o'clock on the night of the fifth, the call came through. Waid says that Sabin seemed in wonderful spirits. He said everything was okay, that Waid was to jump in his plane and get to New York at once."

"He was talking from the cabin here?" Mason asked.

"No, he wasn't. He told Waid the telephone here had gone dead so he'd had to go to a pay station. He didn't say where, and Waid didn't think to ask him. Of course, at the time, it didn't seem particularly important. Waid was in a hurry to get started to New York."

"You've talked with Waid?" Mason asked.

"On the long distance telephone," the sheriff said. "He was still in New York."

"Did he tell the nature of the business?" Mason asked.

"No, he said it was something important and highly confidential. That was all he'd say."

"Waid, I take it, had a chartered plane?" Mason asked.

The sheriff grinned and said, "It looks as though Waid may have cut a corner there. Steve Watkins, who's the son of Sabin's wife by a former marriage, is quite a flyer. He's got a fast plane and likes to fly around the country. I take it Sabin didn't care much for Steve and wouldn't have liked it if he'd known Waid was going to fly back to New York with Steve; but Steve wanted to make the trip and needed the money, so Waid arranged to pay him the charter price and Steve Watkins flew him back."

"What time did they leave?"

"At ten minutes past ten, the night of Monday the fifth," the sheriff said. "Just to make sure, I checked up with the records of the airport."

"And what time did Sabin call Waid?"

"Waid says it wasn't more than ten minutes before he took off. He thinks it was right around ten o'clock."

"He recognized Sabin's voice?" Mason asked.

"Yes, and said Sabin seemed very pleased about some-

22

thing. He told Waid he'd closed the deal and to start at once. He said there'd been a little delay because the telephone here was out of order. He'd had to drive down to a pay station, but he said he was driving right back to the cabin and would be at the cabin for two or three days, that in case Waid encountered any difficulties he was to telephone."

"And Waid didn't telephone?"

"No, because everything went through like clockwork, and Sabin had only told him to telephone in case something went wrong."

Mason said thoughtfully. "Well, let's see then. He was alive at ten o'clock on the evening of Monday, September fifth. Did anyone else see him or talk with him after that?"

"No," the sheriff said. "That's the last time we actually *know* he was alive. From there on, we have to figure evidence. The fishing season opened on Tuesday the sixth. Over there's an alarm clock which had run down. It stopped at two forty-seven. The alarm was set at five-thirty."

"The alarm run down too?" Mason asked.

"Uh-huh."

The telephone bell shattered the silence. The sheriff said, "Excuse me," and scooped up the receiver. He listened a moment, then said, "All right, hold the line," and turned to Mason. "It's for you," he said.

Mason took the receiver and heard Paul Drake's voice at the other end of the line. "Hello, Perry. I took a chance on calling you there. Are you where you can talk?"

"No," Mason said.

"But you can listen all right?"

"Yes. Go ahead. What is it?"

"I think I've found your murderer—at any rate, I've got a lead on that profane parrot, and a swell description of the man that bought him."

"Where?"

"At San Molinas."

"Keep talking," Mason told him.

"A man by the name of Arthur Gibbs runs a pet shop in San Molinas. It's known as the Fifth Avenue Pet Shop.

On Friday the second, a seedy-looking chap came in to buy a parrot in a hurry. Gibbs remembers it, because the man didn't seem to care anything about the parrot except its appearance. Gibbs sold him this profane parrot. He thinks the man didn't know about its habit of cussing . . . I think you'd better talk with Gibbs, Mason."

"Any details?" Mason asked.

"I've got a swell description."

"Does it fit anyone?" Mason inquired.

"No one so far as I can tell," Drake said. ". . . Tell you what I'll do, Perry. I'll go to the Plaza Hotel and wait in the lobby. You get down here as soon as you can. If it's after five-thirty, I'll arrange with Gibbs to wait."

Mason said, "That'll be fine," and hung up the telephone to face the coldly suspicious eyes of Sergeant Holcomb.

Sheriff Barnes, apparently not noticing the interruption, said, "When we broke in here, we found a creel filled with fish. We boxed it up in an air-tight container and sent it to the police laboratory in the city. They report that the creel contained a limit of fish which had been cleaned and wrapped in leaves but hadn't been given a final washing. We've found the remains of his breakfast—a couple of eggs and some bacon rinds. We've found the remains of his lunch—canned beans. The body was clothed in slippers, slacks, and a light sweater. That leather coat there was on the back of the chair. Those are his fishing boots over there with mud on them. There's his fly rod and flies on the table, just as he'd left them when he came in.

"Now, I figure he was killed right around eleven o'clock on the morning of Tuesday the sixth. Would you like to know how I figure it?"

"Very much indeed," Mason said.

Sergeant Holcomb turned on his heel and walked away, showing his silent disgust.

Sheriff Barnes said, "Well, I ain't had much experience in murder cases, but I know how to figure probabilities. I've been in the forest service, and I've worked cattle, and I know how to read trail. I don't know whether the same kind of reasoning will work in a murder case or not, but I don't see why it wouldn't. Anyway, here's the way I figure it. Sabin got up at five-thirty because that's when the alarm went off. He had breakfast of bacon and eggs. He went out fishing. He caught a limit. He got back here, and he was tired and hungry. He didn't even bother to wash the fish and put them in the icebox. He took off his boots, chucked the creel of fish over there, went out into the kitchen and cooked himself some canned beans. There was some coffee in the pot—probably still left from breakfast. He warmed that up.

"The next thing he'd have done was to have given the fish a good washing and put them in the icebox. He was murdered right after lunch and before he'd had a chance to do that. I fixed the time at around eleven o'clock."

"Why not later?" Mason asked.

"Oh, yes," the sheriff said, "I overlooked that. The sun gets on the cabin here about half past ten or eleven and it starts to get warm. It's off the cabin by four o'clock in the afternoon, and it gets cold right away. During the middle of the day it's hot. During the nights it's cold. So I figured he was murdered after it had warmed up and before it had cooled off, but not during the middle of the day when it was real hot. If it had been real cold, he'd have had his coat on and would have lit the fire over there in the fireplace. You see, it's all laid. If it had been real hot, he wouldn't have been wearing his sweater."

"Nice going," Mason said approvingly. "Have you made any experiments to find out how long it takes the alarm clock to run down after it's wound up?"

"I wired the factory," the sheriff said. "They say from around thirty to thirty-six hours, depending on the condition of the clock and how long it's been used.

"Now, here's another thing, Mr. Mason. Whoever killed Sabin was a kindhearted, considerate sort of a guy. Anyway, that's the way I figure it."

He tilted back his hat and scratched the thick hair back of his ears in a characteristic gesture. "Now, you may think it sounds kind of funny for a man to say that about a murderer, but that's the way I figure it just the same. This man had something against Sabin. He wanted to kill him, but he didn't want to kill the parrot. He figured it was apt to be some time before Sabin's body was discovered, and he arranged so the parrot wouldn't starve to death in the meantime.

"Now that makes it look as though the murderer had some powerful reason for wanting Sabin out of the way. It wasn't robbery and it wasn't just sheer cussedness. The murderer was kindhearted. . . if you get what I mean."

"I think I do," Mason said with a smile. "And thank you very much, Sheriff. I won't intrude on you and Sergeant Holcomb longer. I think I understand the situation. I'll walk around the outside of the cabin a couple of times and give it the once-over. I certainly appreciate your courtesy and . . ."

He broke off as someone knocked on the cabin door.

Sheriff Barnes opened the door. A blond, studious-appearing young man in the early thirties peered owlishly from behind horn-rimmed spectacles. "Sheriff Barnes?" he inquired.

"You're Waid?" the sheriff asked.

"Yes."

Sheriff Barnes shook hands. "This is Sergeant Holcomb," he said, "and this is Mr. Mason."

Waid shook hands with each in turn. "I've followed your instructions to the letter, Sheriff," he said. "I got off the plane at Las Vegas. I traveled under an assumed name. I've ditched all the newspaper reporters and . . ."

"Just a minute," Sergeant Holcomb interrupted. "Don't do any talking right now, Waid. Mr. Mason is a lawyer, not an officer. *He's just leaving.*"

Waid suddenly turned to regard Perry Mason with wide eyes. "You're Perry Mason, the lawyer," he said. "Pardon me for not recognizing the name. I've read of your cases, Mr. Mason. I was particularly interested in that one where you acquitted . . ."

"Mason is leaving," Sergeant Holcomb interrupted, "and we'd prefer that you didn't talk with *anyone*, Waid, until you tell us your story."

Waid lapsed into silence with an amused smile flickering at the corners of his mouth.

Mason said, "I'll talk with you some other time, Waid. I'm representing Charles Sabin. Does he know you're here?"

Sergeant Holcomb stepped firmly forward. "That," he said, "is all. There's the door, Mason. Don't let us detain you."

"I won't," Mason assured him with a grin. "The atmosphere here is just a trifle stuffy—or don't you think so, Sergeant?"

Sergeant Holcomb's only retort was to slam the door as Mason stepped out into the glare of the mountain sunlight.

Della Street was seated on the running board of the automobile, making friends with some half-dozen chipmunks. The little animals came almost to her fingertips before turning to scamper away to the comparative safety of a dead pine log, where they chattered their spirits up before slowly creeping back, to approach within a matter of inches. Up in the pine tree above her head a bluejay, apparently thinking she was feeding the chipmunks, fluttered nervously from limb to limb, dropping ever lower, cocking his head from side to side, muttering low throaty squawks of protest at being excluded from the feast—a strange combination of impudence and diffidence.

"Hello, Chief," she said. "Who's the new arrival?"

"Waid, the secretary," Mason replied. "He has something to tell them. That's why they came up here to the cabin. They wanted to meet Waid where no newspaper men would be around . . . And Paul Drake's telephoned he has something hot in San Molinas."

"How about Waid?" she asked. "Going to wait and see if he'll talk, Chief?"

"No. We'll rush to San Molinas. Sergeant Holcomb will warn Waid not to tell me whatever it is he knows, but Charles Sabin will get it out of him later, and then we'll find out. Come on, tell your friends good-by and let's go."

He climbed in behind the steering wheel, started the car, and drove slowly down the driveway which led from the cabin. Once or twice he stopped to look overhead in the branches of the pine tree. "That bluejay," he said, laughing, "is still following us. I wonder if there isn't something I could find to feed him."

"There's some peanut brittle in a bag in the glove

compartment," Della Street said. "You might break a peanut out of that."

"Let's try," Mason said.

He opened the glove compartment, and Della pulled out a paper bag. "Here are a couple of loose peanuts in the bottom of the bag," she told him, and poured them into Mason's cupped hand.

He stood on the running board, held his hands up above his head so that the bluejay could see the shelled peanuts. The jay fluttered noisily from branch to branch, swooped down until he was almost even with Mason's shoulder, then, becoming frightened at his own temerity, zoomed upward with a startled squawk. Twice he repeated this maneuver. The third time, he perched on Mason's hand long enough to grab one of the peanuts in his beak before jumping up, to flutter into the branches of the tree overhead.

Mason, laughing, said, "Gosh, Della, I think I want to do this when *I'm* ready to retire. How nice it would be to have a cabin where you could make friends with . . ."

"What is it, Chief?" she asked, as he broke off abruptly.

Without answering her, Mason strode over to the pine tree in which the bluejay was perched. The jay, thinking he was being pursued, fled into the dark retreat of the forest, his startled squawk being superseded by cries of *"Treason!"* which merged into a more raucous and continuous vituperation of the man who had betrayed his confidence. Della Street, sliding across the seat, her feet pointed at the open door, gave herself impetus by a boost from the steering wheel, and slid to the ground with a quick flash of shapely legs. She ran across to where Mason was standing.

"What is it, Chief?"

Mason said, slowly, "That wire, Della."

"What about it . . . I don't see any . . . Oh, yes . . . . Well, what is it, Chief?"

"I don't know," Mason said. "It isn't an aerial, but you can see the way it's been concealed. It runs along the branch of that limb and is taped to the upper side of it. Then it hits the tree trunk, runs along the tree trunk until it comes to that other limb, goes up through that, runs into this tree, then crosses over to that grove . . . Drive the car outside and park it on the highway, Della. I'm going to take a look."

"What do you think it is, Chief?"

"It looks," he told her, "as though someone had been tapping Fremont Sabin's telephone."

"Gosh, Chief!" she exclaimed. "Isn't *that* something?"

He nodded, but said nothing. He was already walking along under the trees, following the course of the wire so cleverly concealed as to be invisible to any save the most alert observer.

Della Street parked the car on the highway, climbed through a fence, and took a short cut through the pine thicket to join him. A hundred yards away an unpainted cabin was so inconspicuous among the trees that it seemed as much a part of the scenery as the surrounding rocks.

"I think that's the place we're looking for," Mason said, "but we'll trace the wire and find out."

"What do we do when we get there?" she asked.

"It depends," Mason told her. "You'd better stay back, Della, so you can get the sheriff, if the party gets rough."

"Let me stay with you, Chief," she pleaded.

"No," he told her. "Stay back there. If you hear any commotion, beat it for Sabin's cabin as fast as you can, and bring the sheriff."

Mason followed the wire to the place where it abruptly left the protection of the trees to loop itself around insulators just below the eaves of the unpainted cabin. At this point it had been arranged so that it looked very much like the aerial of a wireless set. Mason circled the cabin twice, keeping in the concealment of the dense shadows as much as possible.

Della Street, anxiously watching him from a point some fifty yards distant, moved slowly toward him.

"It's all right," he called to her. "We're going to notify the sheriff." He joined her and they walked back to the cabin where Fred Waner emerged apparently from nowhere to bar their way.

"I want to see the sheriff again," Mason told him.

"All right. You wait here. I'll tell the sheriff you're here."

Waner went to the door of the cabin and called the sheriff. A moment later Sheriff Barnes came out to see what was wanted. When he saw Mason, his face clouded with suspicion. "I thought you'd gone," he said pointedly.

"I started," Mason told him, "and came back. If you can step this way, Sheriff, I think I have something important to show you."

Sergeant Holcomb came to the door of the cabin to stand just behind the sheriff. "What is it?" he asked.

"Something to show the sheriff," Mason replied.

Sergeant Holcomb said grimly, "Mason, if this is a trap to distract our attention, I'll . . ."

"I don't care whether *your* attention's distracted or not," Mason interrupted. "*I'm* talking to the sheriff."

Sergeant Holcomb said to Waner, "Waner, you stay here with Mr. Waid. Don't let him leave. Don't let anyone talk with him. Don't let him touch anything. Do you understand?"

Waner nodded.

"You can count on my co-operation, Sergeant," Waid said with cold formality. "After all, you know, I'm not a criminal. I'm trying to co-operate with you."

"I understand that," Holcomb said, "but whenever Perry Mason. . ."

"What do you have to show us, Mason?" Sheriff Barnes interrupted.

Mason said, "This way, please."

He led the way down the road to where the wire had been tapped under the telephone line. Sergeant Holcomb and the sheriff followed along a few steps behind. "See that?" he asked, pointing upward.

"What?" the sheriff asked.

"That wire."

"It's a telephone wire," Sergeant Holcomb snorted. "What the devil did you think it was, Mason?"

"I'm not talking about that wire," Mason said. "I'm talking about the one which leads off from it. See where it

30

goes through that pine tree where the needles come over and . . ."

"By George, you're right!" the sheriff said. "There *is* a wire!"

"All right," Mason said, "now that you see where the wire is cut in, I'll show you where it runs to," and he led the way over to where he could point out the unpainted cabin, concealed in the trees.

Sergeant Holcomb asked suspiciously, "How did you happen to notice that wire, Mason?"

"I was feeding a bluejay," Mason said. "He took a peanut from my hand, then hopped up in that tree and sat on the limb which carries the wire."

"I see," Holcomb observed in a tone which showed his complete and utter disbelief, "and you just *happened* to see the wire while you were standing under the tree staring up at the bluejay to whom you'd just given a peanut. Is that right?"

"That's right."

"You wanted to see how he'd digest the peanut, I suppose?"

"No, I had another peanut I was going to give him," Mason said patiently. "I wanted him to come down and take it out of my hand."

Sergeant Holcomb said to Sheriff Barnes, "I don't know what his game is, but if Perry Mason is walking down the road feeding peanuts to bluejays, you can gamble there's something back of it. He knew darn well that wire was there, all the time. Otherwise, he'd never have found it."

Sheriff Barnes stared moodily at the cabin. "Keep away," he said, as though entirely oblivious of their conversation. "I'm going into that cabin. Sergeant, if any shooting starts, I leave it to you to back me up."

Quietly, calmly, he approached the door of the cabin, pounded with peremptory knuckles, then lowering his shoulder, smashed his weight against the door. At his third lunge the door gave way and shot backward on its hinges. Sheriff Barnes stepped into the half darkness of the interior to find that Perry Mason was right on his heels, while Sergeant Holcomb was behind Mason, holding his gun in readiness.

"It's all right," the sheriff called, "there's no one here ... You, Mason, shouldn't have taken chances like that."

Mason made no reply. He was staring in frowning contemplation at the array of paraphernalia on the inside of the room. What looked like half of a piece of baggage proved to be a radio amplifier. The whole outfit had been neatly tailored so that, when it was fitted together, it was impossible to distinguish between it and any ordinary piece of baggage. There were headphones, elaborate recording devices, a pencil and pad of paper. A partially smoked cigarette was lying on the edge of a pine table. The cigarette, apparently forgotten, had charred through the wood of the table top. A fine layer of dust had settled over it, as well as over everything else in the room.

"Evidently," the sheriff said, "he ain't been here for quite a spell. But when he left, he lit out in a hurry. He even forgot his cigarette."

"How did you know this was here?" Sergeant Holcomb demanded of Perry Mason, his voice harsh in its implied accusation.

Mason shrugged his shoulders and turned away.

Sheriff Barnes stopped him as he started to walk out. "Say, just a minute, Mason," he said in a quiet tone which was, nevertheless, charged with authority.

Mason stopped.

"Did you know this line had been tapped, Mason?"

"Frankly, Sheriff, I didn't."

"How did you discover it?"

"Just as I told you."

Sheriff Barnes still appeared dubious. Sergeant Holcomb made no attempt to disguise the contemptuous disbelief on his face.

"Did you," Sheriff Barnes asked, "know that Fremont C. Sabin had been back of an attempt to expose organized vice and graft in the Metropolitan Police?"

"Good heavens, no!" Mason said.

Sergeant Holcomb, his face almost a brick-red, said, "I didn't give you that information to be bandied around, Sheriff."

Barnes said, without taking his eyes from Mason, "I'm not bandying it around. You've probably read, Mason, of the confidential advices which the Grand Jury have been receiving, advices which have caused it to start an inquiry against some persons who are prominent politically."

"I've heard something about it," Mason admitted cautiously.

"And you knew that some private citizen was back of this campaign to get information?"

"I'd heard something of the sort."

"Did you have any idea that that person was Fremont C. Sabin?"

Mason said, "Sheriff, I can assure you I didn't have any idea who the person was."

"That's all," Sheriff Barnes said. "I just wanted to be sure, Mason."

"Thanks," Mason said, and walked out, leaving them alone in the cabin.

CHAPTER THREE

PAUL DRAKE was waiting for Mason in the lobby of the Plaza Hotel in San Molinas. He looked at his watch and said, "You're late, Perry, but Gibbs is waiting for us."

Mason said, "Before we go around there, Paul, has anybody else been trying to get in touch with Gibbs?"

"I don't think so. Why?"

"Do you know?"

"No I don't. I hung around there until about an hour ago and then came over here to wait in the hotel. I've been rather expecting you to drive in any time during the last hour."

Mason said, "I was delayed up there because we found that Sabin's line was tapped."

"His line was tapped?"

"Yes. The line into the cabin. The tapping plant may not have been used lately. On the other hand, someone may have been listening in on your conversation with me.

Here's something else. Sabin is the man who's been furnishing finances to the citizens' committee which has been investigating vice conditions and transmitting information on graft to the Grand Jury."

Drake gave a low whistle. "If that's the case," he said, "there were probably anywhere from a hundred to a hundred and fifty people who would have murdered him without batting an eyelash."

"Well, that angle's up to the police. It's too big for us to cover," Mason said.

"You're the boss," Drake said. "We'll go down and talk with Gibbs. He has a swell description of the man who bought the parrot."

"He's certain about the parrot?"

"Yes," Drake said. "I'll let you talk with him, but it's a cinch. He says the man looked a little seedy," Drake continued, "but then, Perry, that's about what you could expect. If any of the vice interests had decided to bump Sabin off, they'd have hired a down-and-outer to do the job, or else would have had a mobster put on the act."

"Would this man know the fellow who bought the parrot if he saw him again?"

"I'll say he would."

"Okay," Mason said, "let's go."

Della Street was waiting in the car at the curb, with the motor running. She said, "Hello, Paul," and handed Mason a newspaper. "Here's the latest afternoon newspaper, Chief, just in from the city. Do you want me to drive?"

"Yes."

"Where is it, Paul?" she asked.

"Straight down this street for three blocks, then turn to the right for two blocks, and swing to the left. It's on a side street, halfway in the block. You should be able to find a parking place in front."

"Okay," she said, and snapped the car into gear. As she slid the big machine out into traffic, Mason opened the newspaper and said, "There probably won't be anything much in here."

"How do they fix the time of death so accurately," Drake asked, "if they didn't find the body for so long?"

"It's quite a story," Mason told him. "Depends on some deduction by the sheriff. He's rather a level-headed chap. I'll tell you about it when we have more time."

He skimmed through the contents of the paper while Della Street drove with swift competency to the pet store.

Mason and Drake alighted. "Want me to stay here, Chief?" Della asked.

"You'd better," Drake said. "You're parked in front of a fireplug. Keep the motor running. We probably won't be long."

Mason handed her the newspaper. "Brush up on current events while we learn about parrots; and quit eating that peanut brittle. It'll spoil your appetite for dinner."

She chuckled. "I was getting along fine until you made me think of that candy; but you're going to have to buy Paul and me dinner on the expense account, Chief, so my loss of appetite may be a blessing in disguise."

They were grinning as they entered the pet store.

Arthur Gibbs was a thin, bald-headed individual with eyes the color of a faded blue shirt which had been left too long on the clothesline. "Hello," he said in a calm, well-modulated voice. "I was just getting ready to close up. I'd about given you up."

"This is Perry Mason," Paul Drake introduced.

Mason extended his hand. Gibbs gave him a bony, long-fingered hand which seemed completely lacking in initiative. As Mason released it, he said, "I suppose you want to know about that parrot."

Mason nodded.

"Well, it's just like I told you," Gibbs said to Paul Drake.

"Never mind what you told me," Paul Drake said. "I want Mr. Mason to get it firsthand. Just go ahead and tell him about it."

"Well, we sold this parrot on the . . ."

"Before you go into that," Drake interrupted, "tell Mr. Mason how you identify the parrot."

"Well," Gibbs said, "of course, I'm just acting on an assumption there. You're asking me about a parrot that cussed whenever it wanted something to eat. I trained a parrot to do that stunt."

"What was the idea?" Mason asked.

"It's just a stunt," Gibbs explained. "Occasionally, you'll find people who think it's smart to have a parrot that cusses. Usually they get tired of them before they've had them a long while, but when they first hear a bird swear, it's quite a novelty."

"And you deliberately train them to swear?" Mason asked.

"Sure. Sometimes a bird will pick up an expression or a sentence just from hearing it once, but for the most part, you have to drill sounds into 'em. Of course, we don't train them to do any real lurid cussing; just a few 'damns' and 'hells' do the trick. People get such a kick out of hearing a parrot cut loose with a good salty line of talk instead of the usual stereotyped 'Polly wants-a-cracker,' they'll buy a bird on the spot."

"All right. When did you sell this bird?"

"Friday, the second of September."

"At what time?"

"Around two or three o'clock in the afternoon, I think it was."

"Tell me about the man who bought it."

"Well, he wore spectacles and had sort of tired eyes. His clothes didn't look any too good, and he looked . . . sort of discouraged . . . no, not discouraged either. Ever since I talked with Mr. Drake about him, I've been trying to think more clearly so I can describe him. He didn't look unhappy. . . . In fact, he seemed to be a man who knew what he was doing and was living his own life in his own way and getting some happiness out of it. He certainly didn't seem to have much money. His suit was shiny, and his elbows were worn almost through, but I will say this for him—he was clean."

"How old?" Mason asked.

"Around fifty-seven or fifty-eight, somewhere around in there."

"Clean-shaven?"

"Yes, he had wide cheekbones and pretty straight lips.

He was about as tall as you are, but he didn't weigh quite as much."

"What was his complexion? Pale or ruddy?" Mason asked.

"He looked like some sort of a rancher," the man said. "He'd been out of doors quite a bit, I think."

"Did he seem nervous or excited?"

"No, he didn't seem as though he'd ever get excited over anything, just calm and quiet. Said he wanted to buy a parrot, and he gave me a description of the sort of bird he wanted to buy."

"What do you mean when you say 'description'?" Mason asked.

"Oh, he told me the breed and size and age."

"Did you have any other birds beside this?"

"No, this was the only one I had that would fit the description."

"Did he hear the bird talk?"

"No, he didn't. That's a funny thing. He just seemed to want a parrot of a certain appearance. He didn't seem to care much about anything else. He took a look at the bird, asked me the price, and said he'd take it."

"Did he buy a cage at the same time?"

"Yes, of course. He took the parrot with him."

"And he was driving a car?"

"That's the thing I can't remember," Gibbs said, frowning. "I can't remember whether I took the cage out to the car or whether he did. I have an impression that he was driving a car, but I didn't pay too much attention to it. If he did have a car, it was just the ordinary sort of a car you'd associate with a man of that type, nothing to attract attention or to impress itself on my memory."

"Did he talk like an educated man?" Mason asked.

"Well, there was something quiet about the way he talked, and he had a peculiar way of looking at you while he was talking . . . looking right straight through you without seeming to be trying to do it. Some people just stare at you, and some seem to try to look holes through you, but this fellow just had a quiet way of . . ."

"Wait a minute," Mason interrupted. "Would you know the man if you saw his picture?"

"Yes, I think I would. I know I'd recognize him if I saw him, and I think I'd recognize the picture if it was a good picture."

Mason said, "Just a minute."

He walked out to where Della Street was sitting in the car. He pulled out his penknife and said, "Going to have to cut your paper to pieces, Della."

"Making dolls?" she asked.

"Making mysteries," he told her, and ran his knife around the border of the newspaper photograph of Fremont C. Sabin. He took it back into the pet store, unfolded the photograph, and said, "Is this, by any chance, the man who bought the parrot?"

Gibbs became excited. "That's the fellow," he said, "that's the man all right. That's a good picture of him; those high cheekbones and that strong, firm mouth."

Mason folded the newspaper photograph and pushed it down in his pocket. He and Drake exchanged significant glances.

"Who was it?" Gibbs asked. "Has his picture been in the paper recently?"

"Just a man who liked parrots," Mason said casually. "Let's wait until after a while to talk about *him*. Now, I want to get some information. Have there been any new parrots sold around here that you know of, recently?"

"I gave everything I had to Mr. Drake," Gibbs said. "But when Mr. Drake was asking me about parrot food this afternoon, and whether I'd had any inquiries from any new people about how to take care of parrots, I couldn't think of any at the time; but after Mr. Drake had left, I happened to remember Helen Monteith."

"And who's Helen Monteith?" Mason asked.

"She's the librarian over at the city library, and a mighty nice girl. Seems to me I read about her being engaged to be married a short time ago. She came in a week or so ago to buy some parrot food and asked me questions about taking care of parrots."

"How long ago?"

"Oh, a week or so. . . . Let me see, yes, it's been a little more than a week, maybe ten days."

"Did she tell you that she'd bought a parrot?"

"No, she didn't; just asked some questions about parrots."

"Did you ask her why she wanted to know?"

"I may have. I can't remember now. The whole thing is kind of fuzzy in my memory. You know how it is; a man doesn't think very much about all of those little transactions. Thinking back on it now, I can remember that at the time I wondered whether she'd been in the city and bought a parrot in there. . . . Come to think of it, I guess I didn't ask her any questions at all, just gave her what she wanted."

"Do you have her address?"

"I can find it in the phone book," Gibbs said.

"Don't bother," Mason said, "we'll look it up. You'd better shut up shop and go home. . . . She's listed in the telephone book, is she?"

"I think so. If she isn't, it's a cinch she's listed in the city directory. Here, let me look her up."

Gibbs ran the pages of a thick, blue book through his long, listless fingers, then said, "Here it is, 219 East Wilmington Street. You go out Main Street ten blocks and come to a wide street. That's Washington. The next street on the other side is Wilmington. Turn to the right and go for two blocks, and you'll be right near the place."

Mason said, "Thanks. I wonder if we can compensate you in any way for your trouble. . . ."

"Not at all," Gibbs said. "I'm glad to do it."

"Well, we certainly appreciate it."

"You don't know whether we'd find Miss Monteith at the library now, or whether she'd be at her residence, do you?" Drake asked.

Before the man could answer, Mason said, "I don't think that angle is particularly important, Paul. After all, it's just a matter of someone asking a casual question. Good Lord, if we're going to try to run down everyone who orders parrot food, we'll be working on this thing for a year." He turned to Gibbs with a smile and said, "It looked as though we were on the track of something, but the way it's turning out now, I guess it doesn't amount to much."

He took Paul Drake's arm and led him to the door.

When they were out on the sidewalk, Drake said, "What was the idea, Perry? He might have given us a little more information."

"Not much more," Mason said, "and I don't want to let him think we consider this as being too important. Later on he's going to read his afternoon newspaper. Then, if he thinks we struck a hot trail, he'll tell the police, and . . ."

"That's right," Drake interrupted. "I'd overlooked that."

"What luck?" Della Street asked.

"Plenty," Mason said, "but whether it's good, bad, or indifferent is more than we know yet. Swing over to Main Street and run out until after you've passed Washington, then turn to the right on the next block. We'll tell you where to stop."

She touched two fingers of her right hand to the abbreviated rim of her tilted hat. "Aye, aye, sir," she said, and started the car.

"We don't want to try the library first?" Drake asked. "It's probably nearer."

"No," Mason said. "A woman wouldn't keep a parrot in a library. She'd keep it in her home."

"Do you think she's keeping a parrot?"

"I wouldn't be surprised. I'll tell you more about it within the next ten or fifteen minutes."

Della Street swung the car skillfully through the late afternoon traffic. Drake, with his head pushed outside the car, reading street signs, said, "That's Washington, Della, the next is the one we want."

"There's no sign on this corner," Della said as she slowed the car.

"I think it's the corner we want," Mason told her. "Go ahead and make the turn anyway. . . . Good Lord, I don't know why it is that a city will go to all sorts of trouble and expense to attract tourists and strangers with advertising, and then act on the assumption that only the natives, who know every street in the city, are going to be looking for residences. It wouldn't cost much to put up a sign big enough to read on every street intersection of any importance. . . . This is it, Della, pull in to the curb."

The house was a small California bungalow which

dated back to an era of older and cheaper buildings. The outside consisted of redwood boards with strips of batten nailed across the cracks. Back of the house was a small garage, the doors of which stood open, disclosing an interior which was evidently used as a wood-shed and storehouse.

As Mason got out of the car, a parrot squawked in a high, shrill voice. "Hello, hello. Come in and sit down."

Mason grinned at Drake. "Well," he said, "I guess we've found *a* parrot."

"There he is," Della Street said, "in a cage on the screen porch."

"Do we go to the front door and interview Helen Monteith?" Drake asked

"No," Mason said, "We go to the back door and interview the parrot."

He walked directly across the strip of dry grass which had evidently been a lawn at one time, until lack of care and the long Southern California dry spell had forced it to give up the struggle for existence. The parrot, in a bell-shaped cage on the screen porch, executed a peculiar double shuffle on the round perch of the cage. His feet fairly streaked back and forth in excitement as he squawked, "Come in and sit down. Come in and sit down. Hello, hello. Come in and sit down."

Mason said, "Hello, Polly," and went up close to the screen.

"Hello, Polly," the bird replied.

Mason pointed at the parrot. "Oh, oh," he said.

"What?" Drake asked.

"Look at the right foot. One of the toes is gone," Mason said.

The parrot, as though mocking him, burst into high, shrill laughter; then, evidently in high good humor, preened his glossy, green feathers, smoothing them carefully between the upper hooked beak and the surface of the black-coated tongue. Abruptly, the bird turned its wicked glittering eyes on Perry Mason. It ruffled its feathers as though showing great excitement and suddenly squawked, "Put down that gun, Helen! Don't shoot! *Squawk. Squawk.* My God, you've shot me!"

The parrot paused and cocked its head on one side as though seeking by a survey of the three startled faces lined up in front of the screen to estimate the sensation its words had produced.

"Good Lord," Drake said. "Do you suppose . . ."

He broke off as a woman's voice said, "Good evening. What was it you wanted, please?"

They turned to see a matronly woman with broad, capable shoulders staring curiously at them.

"I'm looking for a Miss Monteith," Mason said. "Does she live here?"

The woman inquired, with just a trace of reproof in her voice, "Have you been to the front door?"

"No, we haven't," Mason admitted. "We parked the car out here at the curb and saw the garage was empty. . . . Then I became attracted by the parrot. I'm interested in parrots."

"May I ask your name?"

"Mason," the lawyer told her, "Mr. Mason, and may I inquire yours?"

"I'm Mrs. Winters. I'm Helen Monteith's next-door neighbor, only her name isn't Monteith any more."

"It isn't?"

"No. She was married almost two weeks ago . . . a man by the name of Wallman, George Wallman, a book-keeper."

"Do you," Mason asked, "happen to know how long she's had the parrot?"

"I believe the parrot was a present from her husband. She's had it for almost two weeks. Did you have some business with Mrs. Wallman?"

"Just wanted to see her and ask her a few questions," Mason said with his most disarming manner, and as Mrs. Winters looked at the other two as though expecting an introduction, Mason detached himself from the group and took her to one side where he could lower his voice in confidence. Della Street, interpreting his tactics, touched Paul Drake with her elbow, and they walked back to the automobile, got in and sat down.

Mason asked, "How long has Mrs. Wallman been gone, Mrs. Winters?"

"About half or three quarters of an hour, I guess."

"You don't know where she went or when she expects to be back, do you?"

"No, I don't. She came home in an awful hurry and ran across the lawn to the house. I don't think she was in the house over two or three minutes, then she came tearing out and got her car out of the garage."

"Didn't she drive up in her own car?" Mason asked.

"No, she doesn't usually take her car to work with her. It's only eight or ten blocks and, when it's nice, she walks to work."

"How did she come home?" Mason asked her.

"In a taxi. I don't know what she intends to do about the parrot. She didn't say a word to me about giving him food or water. I guess there's plenty in the cage to last him over night, but I don't know how long she intends to be gone. . . . I must close those garage doors for her. She never leaves them open when she takes the car out, but today she didn't stop for anything, just backed the car out of the garage, and went a-kiting down the street."

"Probably had a date in the city for a theater or something," Mason said. "Perhaps she was meeting her husband. . . . I take it her husband wasn't with her."

"No. I believe he's out somewhere looking for work—he comes and goes. She spent the weekend with him somewhere I know, because I had to keep the parrot for her."

"Her husband's out of work?" Mason asked.

"Yes."

"Quite a few people are these days," Mason told her, "but I suppose a young man who has plenty of vitality and stick-to-it-iveness can . . ."

"But he isn't young," Mrs. Winters interrupted, with the air of one who could be led to say more if properly encouraged.

"Why, I gathered she was a young woman," Mason said. "Of course, I haven't met her personally, but . . ."

"Well, it depends on what you call young. She's in the early thirties. The man she married must be twenty years older than she is. I guess he's steady enough and nice enough and all that, but what in the world a young

43

woman wants to go and tie herself up for, with a man old enough to be her father . . . There, I mustn't go gossiping. I suppose it's none of *my* business. After all, *she* married him, *I* didn't. I made up my mind when she introduced him to me that I wasn't going to say a word to her about his age. I figure it's just none of my business, and I'm a great body to mind my own business. . . . May I ask what you want to see Mrs. Wallman about?"

Mason said, "I wanted to see Mrs. Wallman, but I also wanted to see her husband. You don't know where I could reach him, do you?"

Her eyes glittered with suspicion. "I thought," she said, "you didn't know she was married."

"I didn't," Mason admitted, "when I came here, but now that I've found it out, I'm quite anxious to see her husband. I . . . I might have a job for him."

"There's a lot of younger men out of jobs these days," Mrs. Winters said. "I don't know what Helen was thinking of, taking on a man like that to support, because that's just what it's going to amount to. I guess he's a nice, quiet, respectable man and all that, but after all he's out of work, and if you ask me, his clothes show it. I *would* think Helen'd get him a new suit of clothes. She lives simple enough and they do say as how she has quite a little put by for a rainy day."

Mason's eyes narrowed in thoughtful speculation. Abruptly he fished in his vest pocket with his thumb and forefinger and took out the folded newspaper picture of Fremont C. Sabin. "Is there any chance," he asked, showing Mrs. Winters the picture, "that this photograph is of her husband?"

Mrs. Winters carefully adjusted her glasses, took the newsprint picture from Mason, and held it up so that the western light fell full upon it.

In the automobile, Paul Drake and Della Street watched breathlessly.

An expression of surprise came over Mrs. Winters' face. "Land sakes, yes," she said. "That's the man, just as natural as life. I'd know him anywhere. Good Lord, what's George Wallman done to get *his* picture in the newspapers?"

Mason retrieved the picture. "Look here, Mrs. Winters," he said, "it's vitally important that I find Mrs. Wallman at once and ..."

"Oh, you want to see *Mrs*. Wallman now. Is that it?"

"Either Mr. or Mrs.," Mason said. "Since she was the last one you've seen, perhaps you could tell me where I'd be able to find her."

"I'm sure I don't know. She might have gone to visit her sister. Her sister's a school teacher in Edenglade."

"Is her sister married?" Mason asked.

"No, she's never been married."

"Then her name is Monteith?"

"Yes, Sarah Monteith. She's a couple of years older than Helen, but she looks about fifteen years older. She's painfully correct in her ways. She takes life too seriously and ..."

"You don't know of any other relatives?" Mason asked.

"No."

"And no other place where she would have gone?"

"No."

Mason terminated the interview by raising his hat with elaborate politeness. "Well, Mrs. Winters," he said, "I certainly thank you for your co-operation. I'm sorry that I bothered you. After all, I guess I'll have to plan on seeing Mrs. Wallman some other time."

He turned back toward the car.

"You can leave a message with me," Mrs. Winters said. "I'll see that she gets it and ... but ..."

"I'm afraid I'll have to see her personally," Mason said, jumping into the car and signaling for Della Street to drive on.

"Put down that gun, Helen!" the parrot on the porch screamed. "Don't shoot! *Squawk. Squawk*. My God, you've shot me!"

Della Street lurched the car into motion.

Mason said, "Okay, Paul, find her. Get out and start using the telephone. Spread operatives all over the country. Get a description of her car and the license number from the Motor Vehicle Department or from the Assessor's Office or wherever you can. Try the sister in Edenglade."

"Where are you going?" Drake asked.

"I'm heading for Sabin's place in town," Mason told him. "I think the chances are about even that she's headed there, and I want to beat her to it if I can."

"What do I do with her if I find her?" Drake asked.

"Put her where no one can talk with her until after I do."

"That," Drake said, "is something of a large order, Perry."

"Oh, shucks," Mason told him, "don't be so squeamish. Put her in a sanitarium somewhere as suffering from a nervous breakdown."

"She's probably upset," Drake told him, "but we'd have quite a job making the nervous breakdown business stick."

"Not if she realized the full significance of what that parrot's saying, you wouldn't," Mason said grimly.

CHAPTER FOUR

MASON guided his car in close to the curb and glanced across the street at the lighted house. "Certainly is big enough," he said to Della Street. "No wonder the old man got lonely living there."

He had slid out from behind the wheel and was standing at the curb, locking the car door, when Della Street said, "I think this is one of Paul Drake's men coming."

Mason looked up to see a man emerge from the shadows, glance at the license plate on the automobile, then cut across the beam of illumination from the headlights.

"Shall I put the lights out, Chief?" Della Street asked.

"Please," he told her.

The light switch clicked the surroundings into darkness. The man approached Mason and said, "You're Mason, aren't you?"

"Yes," Mason told him. "What is it?"

"I'm from the Drake agency. The old woman and her son got in on the plane this afternoon. They came directly here. Another operative is tailing them. They're inside now, and there's a hell of a row going on."

Mason looked across at the huge house silhouetted against the night sky, its windows glowing in subdued brilliance through the drapes.

"Well," he said, grinning, "I may as well go on in and join the fight."

The operative said, "The boss telephoned for us to be on the lookout for a car with license number 1V-1302. I saw you drive up and thought maybe that was the bus I was looking for."

Mason said, "No, that's probably Helen Monteith's car. She lives in San Molinas, and she may come to the house here. I want to see her just as soon as we can . . ."

He broke off as a car swung around the corner, and headlights cast moving shadows along the street.

"I'll see who this is," the detective said. "Probably some more relatives coming in to join the family row."

He walked around the rear of Mason's machine, then came running back and said, "That's the license number the boss told us to be on the lookout for. Do you want it?"

Mason's answer was to start running for the place where the car was being backed into a vacant space at the curb. By the time the young woman who was driving it had switched off her headlights and stepped from the car, Mason was abreast of her.

"I want to talk with you, Miss Monteith," he said.

"Who are you?" she asked sharply.

"Mason is the name," he said. "I'm a lawyer, representing Charles Sabin."

"What do you want with me?"

"I want to talk with you."

"What about?"

"About Fremont C. Sabin."

"I don't think I have anything to say."

"Don't be silly," Mason told her. "The thing has gone so far now it's entirely out of your hands."

"What do you mean?"

"I mean that the newspaper men are on the job. It isn't going to take *them* long to find out that you claim to have gone through a marriage ceremony with Fremont C. Sabin, who was going under the name of George Wallman. After they've gone that far, they'll find out that Sabin's parrot, Casanova, is on the screen porch of your house in San Molinas, and that since the murder he's been saying, 'Drop that gun, Helen. . . . Don't shoot. . . . My God, you've shot me.' "

She was tall enough so that she needed to raise her eyes only slightly to meet the lawyer's. She was slender enough to be easy and graceful in her motions, and her posture indicated a self-reliance and ability to reach decisions quickly, and put them into rapid execution.

"How," she asked, apparently without batting an eyelash, "did *you* find out all this?"

"By using the same methods the police and the newspapermen will use," Mason said.

"Very well," she told him quietly, "I'll talk. What do you want to know?"

"Everything," he said.

"Do you," she asked, "want to talk in my car, or in the house?"

"In my car," Mason told her, "if you don't mind."

He cupped his hand under her elbow, escorted her back to his automobile, introduced Della Street, and placed Helen Monteith beside him in the front seat.

"I want you to understand," Helen Monteith said, "that I've done nothing wrong—nothing of which I am ashamed."

"I understand," Mason told her.

He could see her profile outlined against the illumination which filtered in through the car windows. Her manner was quick, alert, intelligent; her voice was well controlled. She evidently had ample speaking range to make her voice expressive when she chose, yet she resorted to no tricks of emphasis or expression to win sympathy. She spoke rapidly, and managed to convey the impression that, regardless of what her personal feelings in the matter might be, she was keeping her emotions entirely divorced from those events which she considered it necessary to report.

"I'm a librarian," she said, "employed in the San Molinas library. For various reasons, I have never married. My position gives me at once an opportunity to cultivate a taste for the best in literature, and to learn something of character. I have nothing in common with the younger set who find alcoholic stimulation the necessary prerequisite to any attempt at conversation or enjoyment.

"I first met the man whom I now know as Fremont C. Sabin about two months ago. He entered the library, asked for books dealing with certain economic subjects. He told me he never read newspapers because they were merely a recital of crimes and political propaganda. He read news magazines for his general information, was interested in history, economics, science and biographies. He read some of the best fiction. His questions and comments were unusually intelligent, and the man impressed me. I realized, of course, that he was much older than I, and, quite apparently, was out of work. His clothes were well-kept, but had seen far better days. I'm dwelling on this because I want you to understand the situation."

Mason nodded.

"He told me his name was George Wallman; that he had been employed as a grocery clerk, had saved a little money, and purchased a store of his own; that, after making a living out of it for several years, he found himself forced out of business by a combination of unfortunate circumstances. His original capital was gone. He had tried to get work and was unable to find any because, as he had been so frequently told, not only were there no jobs, but in the event there had been, employers would prefer to fill them with younger men."

"You had no inkling of his real identity?" Mason asked.

"None whatever."

"Do you know why he chose to assume this fictitious personality?" Mason asked.

"Yes," she said shortly.

"Why?"

"I realize now," she said, "that, in the first place, the

49

man was married; in the second place, he was wealthy. He was trying to protect himself from an unpleasant wife on the one hand, and avaricious gold-diggers or black-mailers on the other."

"And apparently, somewhere in the process, he messed up your life pretty well," Mason said sympathetically.

She turned on him, not in anger, but with quick resentment. "That," she said, "shows that you didn't know George . . . Mr. Sabin."

"It's a fact, isn't it?" Mason asked.

She shook her head. "I don't know what the complete explanation is," she said, "but you can rest assured that when all the facts are uncovered, his reasons will have been good ones."

"And you feel no bitterness?" the lawyer inquired.

"None whatever," she said, and for a moment there was a wistful note in her voice. "The happiest two months of my life were in the period following my meeting with Mr. Sabin. All of this tragedy has hit me a terrific blow. . . . However, you're not interested in my grief."

"I'm trying to understand," he said gently.

"That's virtually all there is to it," she said; "I had some money which I'd saved from my salary. I recognized, of course, that it was hopeless for a man in the late fifties, who had no particular skill in any profession, and no regular trade, to get employment. I told him that I would back him in starting a grocery store in San Molinas. He looked the town over, but finally came to the conclusion that it wouldn't be possible to make a go of things there. So then I told him to pick his place."

"Then what?" Mason asked.

"Then," she said, "he went out to look the territory over."

"You heard from him?" Mason asked.

"Letters, yes."

"What did he say in his letters?"

"He was rather vague about matters pertaining to business," she said; "his letters were—mostly personal. We had been married less than a week when he left." She turned suddenly to face Mason and said, "And regardless of what else may transpire, he loved me."

She said it simply, without dramatic emphasis, without allowing her personal grief to intrude upon the statement. It was merely a statement of facts made as a calm assertion by one who knows whereof she speaks.

Mason nodded silent acquiescence.

"The first intimation I had," she said, "was . . . was . . . this afternoon, when I picked up the afternoon paper and saw his picture as Fremont C. Sabin, the man who had been murdered."

"You recognized him at once?"

"Yes. There had been certain things which hadn't been exactly . . . consistent with the character he had assumed. Since our marriage, I had found myself watching him with a vague uneasiness, because the man simply didn't fit into the character of a failure. He was a man who couldn't have failed at anything in life; he had too much quiet force of character, too much intelligence, too much native shrewdness; and he seemed too reluctant to touch any of my money. He kept putting that off, saying that he had a little money of his own saved up, and that we'd use that to live on until it was gone, and then he'd take mine."

"But you didn't suspect that he really had great wealth?" Mason asked.

"No," she said, "I hadn't crystallized any of the doubts in my mind into even being doubts. They were simply little things which remained lodged in my memory, and then, when I saw his picture in the paper, and read the account of his death, those things all clicked into place. I'd been prepared for it in a way when I read in the morning paper about the mountain cabin . . . and saw the photographs of that cabin."

"Of course," Mason said, "you'd been without letters for the past week?"

"On the contrary," she said, "I had received a letter from him only this Saturday, the tenth. It had been mailed from Santa Delbarra. He said he was negotiating for a lease on what seemed to be an ideal storeroom. He seemed to be very enthusiastic, and said he hoped to be back within a few days."

"I presume," Mason said, "you aren't entirely familiar with his handwriting, and . . ."

"I feel quite certain," she said, "that the writing is that of Mr. Sabin . . . or George Wallman, as I knew him."

"But," Mason said, "the evidence shows that the body was lying in that cabin—you'll forgive me for being brutally frank, Miss Monteith, but it's necessary—the evidence shows that he was murdered on September sixth."

"Can't you understand?" she said wearily. "He was testing my love. He wanted to keep in the character of Wallman until he knew I loved *him* and wasn't after money. He wasn't looking for any lease. He planted these letters and left them to be mailed from various places on different dates."

"You have that last letter?" Mason asked.

"Yes."

"May I see it?"

She made as though to open her purse, then shook her head and said, "No."

"Why not?"

"The letter is personal," she said. "I understand that, to a certain extent, my privacy must of necessity be invaded by authorities making an investigation, but I am not going to surrender his letters, unless it becomes absolutely imperative."

"It's going to become imperative," Mason said. "If he left letters with someone to be mailed at various times and places, that someone may have been the last person to have seen him alive."

She remained silent.

"When were you married?" Mason asked.

"August twenty-seventh."

"Where?"

She hesitated a moment, then tilted her chin and said, "We crossed the border into Mexico and were married there."

"May I ask why?"

"George . . . Mr. Sabin said that for certain reasons he preferred to be married there . . . and . . ."

"Yes?" Mason prompted as she stopped.

"We were to be married again," she said, "in Santa Delbarra."

"Why there?"

"He . . . he intimated that his former wife had secured a divorce, that the interlocutory decree had not yet become final, and there might be some doubt as to the validity of the marriage. He said that it would . . . After all, Mr. Mason, this is something of a private matter."

"It is in part," Mason said, "and in part it isn't."

"Well, you can look at it in this way. I knew at the time I married him that the marriage was of doubtful legality. I considered it as a . . . as a gesture to the conventions. I understood that it would be followed with a second and more legal marriage that was to have taken place very shortly."

"Then you thought your first marriage was illegal?"

"No," she said, "I thought that it was legal . . . Well, when I say it was of doubtful legality, I mean that it was a marriage which would have been illegal if it had been performed in this country. . . . That's rather difficult to explain . . . and I don't know that I care to try."

"How about the parrot?" Mason asked.

"My hus— Mr. Sabin had always wanted a parrot."

"I understand that. How long had the parrot been with you?"

"Mr. Sabin brought him home on Friday, the second, I believe it was. It was two days before he left."

Mason stared in frowning contemplation at the determined profile. "Did you," he asked, "know that Mr. Sabin purchased this parrot in San Molinas?"

"Yes."

"What's the parrot's name?"

"Casanova."

"Did you read about the parrot which was found in the mountain cabin?"

"Yes."

"Do you know anything about that parrot?"

"No."

Mason frowned and said, "You know, Miss Monteith, this just doesn't make sense."

"I understand that," she admitted readily enough. "That's why I think it's a mistake to try and judge Mr.

Sabin by what has happened. It means we simply haven't all the facts."

"Do you know anything about that mountain cabin?" Mason asked.

"Yes, of course, we spent our honeymoon there. My hus— Mr. Sabin said that he knew the owner of the cabin, and had arranged to borrow it for a few days. Looking back on it now I can realize how absurd it was to think that this man who claimed to be out of a job and . . . Oh, well, he had his reasons for doing what he did, and I respect those reasons."

Mason started to say something, then checked himself and frowned thoughtfully for several silent seconds. "How long were you at the cabin?" he asked at length.

"We just stayed there over the weekend. I had to be back on my job Monday night."

"You were married in Mexico, and then drove to the cabin?"

"Yes."

"And did your husband seem to know his way around the cabin pretty well—that is, be familiar with it?"

"Oh, yes, he told me that he'd spent a month there once."

"Did he tell you the name of the man who owned the cabin?"

"No."

"And you made no attempt to find out?"

"No."

"You were married on the twenty-seventh of August?"

"Yes."

"And you arrived at the cabin on the evening of the twenty-seventh?"

"No, the morning of the twenty-eighth. It was too long a drive to make that first night."

"You left some clothes there?"

"Yes."

"Did you do that deliberately?"

"Yes, we left rather hurriedly. One of the neighbors came to call, and Mr. Sabin didn't want to see him. I suppose he didn't want the neighbor to know about me—

54

or was afraid I'd learn his real identity through the neighbor. Anyway, he didn't answer the door, and then we hurried into the car and left. Mr. Sabin told me that no one else would be using the cabin, and that we'd return sometime within the next month."

"During the time you were there in the cabin, did Mr. Sabin use the telephone?"

"He put through two calls."

"Do you know whom the calls were to? Did you listen to the conversation?"

"No."

"Do you have any idea who might have killed him, any inkling whatever as to . . ."

"Not the slightest."

"And I don't suppose," Mason went on casually, "that you know anything about the weapon with which the murder was committed?"

"Yes," she said unexpectedly, "I do."

"You do?"

"Yes."

"What about it?" Mason asked.

"That weapon," she said slowly, "is part of a collection at the San Molinas Public Library."

"There's a collection of guns there?"

"Yes, there's a museum in one room, in connection with the library—that is, it isn't exactly operated in connection with the library, but it was presented to the city, and, under an arrangement with the library committee, the librarian has charge of the room. The janitor, who takes care of the library, does janitor work, and . . ."

"Who took this gun from the collection?"

"I did."

"Why?"

"My husband asked me to. He . . . No, I don't think I'm going to talk about that, Mr. Mason."

"To whom did you give this gun?"

"I think we'll just skip everything about the gun."

"When did you first know your husband was really Fremont C. Sabin?"

"This morning, when I saw the picture of the cabin in the paper . . . well, I suspected it then. I didn't know what to do. I just waited, hoping against hope. Then the afternoon papers published his picture. Then I knew."

Mason asked abruptly, "Just what do you have to gain in a financial way?"

"What do you mean?"

"Was there any will, any policy of insurance, any . . ."

"No, of course not," she interrupted.

Mason stared thoughtfully at her. "What are your plans?" he asked.

"I'm going in and meet Mr. Sabin's son. I'm going to explain the circumstances to him."

"His wife is in there now," Mason said.

"You mean Fremont C. Sabin's wife?"

"Yes."

She bit her lip, then sat silently digesting that bit of information.

Mason said gently, "You know, Miss Monteith, the authorities are not going to understand how that gun happened to be one to which you had access . . . Look here, you didn't find out, by any chance, who he was, and find out about his wife, and get angry because . . ."

"You mean and kill him?" she interrupted.

"Yes," Mason said.

"The very thought is absurd! I loved him. I have never loved any man . . ." she broke off.

"He was," Mason pointed out, "considerably older than you."

"And wiser," she said, "and gentler, and more considerate, and . . . You have no idea how grand he was; contrasted with the young men whom I meet around the library—the fresh ones who try to take me out, the stupid ones, the ones who have lost all ambition . . ." Her voice trailed away into silence.

Mason turned to Della Street. "Della," he said, "I want you to take Miss Monteith with you. I want you to keep her some place where she won't be annoyed by newspapermen, do you understand?"

"I think I do," Della Street said quietly from the back seat, and her voice sounded as though she had been crying.

"I don't want to go anywhere," Miss Monteith said. "I

understand that I'm in for a disagreeable ordeal. The only thing I can do is face it."

"Do you want to meet Mrs. Sabin?" Mason asked. "I understand that she's rather disagreeable."

"No," Helen Monteith said shortly.

Mason said, "Miss Monteith, I think the developments of the next few hours may make a great deal of difference. Right at present the police haven't identified that murder weapon; that is, they haven't found out where it came from. When they do . . . well, you're going to be arrested, that's all."

"You mean and charged with murder?"

"You'll be booked on suspicion of murder."

"But that's absurd."

"It isn't absurd, looking at it from the police viewpoint," Mason said. "It isn't even absurd looking at it from any common-sense reconstruction of the evidence."

She was silent for a few seconds, thinking over what he had said, then she turned to him and asked, "Just whom do you represent?"

"Charles Sabin."

"And what are you trying to do?"

Mason said, "Among other things, I'm trying to clear up this murder case. I'm trying to find out what happened."

"What is your interest in me?"

"You," Mason told her, "are in a spot. My training has been to sympathize with the underdog and fight for him."

"But I'm not an underdog."

"You will be by the time that family gets done with you," Mason told her grimly.

"You want me to run away?"

"No, that's exactly what I *don't* want. If the situation hasn't clarified itself by tomorrow, we'll . . . well, we'll cross that bridge when we come to it."

She reached her decision. "Very well," she said, "I'll go."

Mason said to Della Street, "You'll go in her car, Della."

"Shall I communicate with you, Chief?" she asked.

"No," Mason said. "There are some things I want to find out, and other things I don't want to know anything about."

"I get you, Chief," she said. "Come on, Miss Monteith. We haven't any time to waste around here."

Mason stood on the curb, watching the car, until the tail-light became a red pin-point in the distance. Then he turned toward the huge, gloomy house with its somber atmosphere of massive respectability.

CHAPTER FIVE

RICHARD WAID, the secretary, opened the door in response to Mason's ring. His face showed his relief at seeing the lawyer. "C.W. has been trying to get you on the phone," he said. "I've been calling every few minutes."

"Something wrong?" Mason inquired.

"Mrs. Sabin is home—the widow."

"Has that resulted in complications?" the lawyer asked.

"I'll say it has. Listen, you can hear them in there now."

Richard Waid stood slightly to one side, and the sound of a woman's excited voice came pouring through the doorway. The words were undistinguishable, but there could be no mistaking the harsh, rasping sound of the voice itself.

"Well," Mason said, "perhaps I'd better join in the fight."

"I wish you would," Waid said, and then, after a moment, "It may be that you can tone her down a bit."

"Does she have a lawyer?" Mason asked.

"Not yet. She's threatening to hire all the lawyers in the city."

"Threatening?" Mason inquired.

"Yes," Waid said shortly, and as he led the way into the living room, added, "And that's putting it mildly."

Charles Sabin got to his feet at once, as Mason entered. He came forward to grasp the lawyer's hand, with evident relief. "You must be a mind reader, Mr. Mason," he said. "I've been trying to get you for the last half hour."

He turned and said, "Helen, let me present Perry Mason. Mrs. Helen Watkins Sabin, Mr. Mason."

Mason bowed. "I am pleased to meet you, Mrs. Sabin."

She glared at him as though he had been an insect impaled with a pin and mounted on a wall board. "Humph!" she said.

She was heavy, but there was nothing flabby about her heaviness. Her body was hard beef, and her eyes held the arrogant steadiness of a person who is accustomed to put others on the defensive and keep them there.

"And her son, Mr. Watkins, Mr. Mason."

Watkins came forward to take Mason's hand in a firm, cordial grasp. His eyes sought those of the lawyer, and his voice as he said, "I'm *very* glad to meet you, Mr. Mason," lent emphasis to his words. "I've been reading so much about you, from time to time, that it's a real pleasure to meet you in the flesh. I was particularly interested in the newspaper accounts of the trial of that case involving the murder of the insurance man."

"Thank you very much," Mason said, letting his eyes take in the bulging forehead, the well-rounded cheeks, the steady blue eyes, and the fit of the well-pressed flannels.

"I've had quite a trip," Steve Watkins said by way of explanation. "I flew from New York down to Central America to pick up mother, and came back with her. Haven't even tubbed yet."

"Did you fly your own plane?" Mason asked.

"No, I didn't, although I do quite a bit of flying. But my job wasn't exactly tuned up for a long flight. I went on a passenger plane to Mexico City, and then chartered a private plane down and back. We had another plane fly down to wait for us in Mexico City."

"You *have* had quite a trip," Mason agreed.

Mrs. Sabin said, "Never mind the personal amenities, Steve. I see no occasion to waste time trying to meet Mr.

59

Mason on friendly terms. You know perfectly well he's going to try to knife us. We may just as well start our fight and get it over with."

"Fight?" Mason asked.

She pushed forward her chin aggressively and said, "I said 'fight.' *You* should know what the word means."

"And what," Mason asked, "are we going to fight about?"

"Don't beat around the bush," she said, "it isn't like you—not from all I've heard, and I don't want to be disappointed in you. Charles has employed you to see that I'm jockeyed out of my rights as Fremont's wife. I don't intend to be jockeyed."

Mason said, "Perhaps in the circumstances, Mrs. Sabin, if you retained your attorney, and let me discuss matters with him . . ."

"I'll do that when I get good and ready," she said. "I don't need any lawyer—not right now. When I need one I'll get one."

Steve Watkins said, "Just a minute, Moms, Uncle Charles only said that . . ."

"Shut up," Mrs. Sabin snapped, "I'm running this. I heard what Charles said. All right, Mr. Mason, what have you to say for yourself?"

Mason dropped into a chair, crossed his long legs, grinned across at Charles Sabin, and said nothing.

"All right, then, *I'll* say something. I've told Charles Sabin, and now I'm telling you. I know only too well that Charles has resented me ever since I married into this family. If I had told Fremont one half of the things that I've had to put up with, Fremont would have had Charles on the carpet. He wouldn't have stood for it for a minute. Regardless of what Charles may think, Fremont loved me. Charles was so afraid that some of the property was going to get away from him, that he was completely blinded by prejudice. As a matter of fact, if he'd been disposed to be fair with me, I might have been fair with him now. As it is, I'm in the saddle, and I'm going to do the driving. Do you understand, Mr. Mason?"

"Perhaps," Mason said, lighting a cigarette, "you could explain a little more clearly, Mrs. Sabin."

60

"Very well, I will explain clearly. I'm Fremont's widow. I *think* there's a will leaving the bulk of his property to me. He told me he was making such a will. If there is a will I'm the executrix of it; if there isn't, I'm entitled to letters of administration. In any event, I am going to be in charge of the estate, and I don't want any interference from any of the relatives."

"You haven't the will with you?" Mason asked.

"Certainly not. I'm not in the habit of carrying my husband's wills around with me. I presume it's in his papers somewhere, unless Charles has destroyed it. And in case you don't know it, Mr. Mason, Charles Sabin is perfectly capable of doing just that."

Mason said, "Can't we leave the personalities out of it, Mrs. Sabin?"

She stared defiantly at him, and said simply, "No."

Richard Waid started to say something, then checked himself.

Mason said, "Look here, Mrs. Sabin, I want to ask you a personal question. Hadn't you and Mr. Sabin separated?"

"What do you mean by that?"

"Just what I say. Hadn't you separated, hadn't you decided that you were not going to live together any longer as man and wife? Wasn't your trip around the world in accordance with such an understanding?"

"Absolutely not, that's ridiculous."

"Didn't you have an agreement with Mr. Sabin by which you were to get a divorce?"

"Absolutely not."

Waid said, "Really, Mr. Mason, I . . ."

He broke off as Mrs. Sabin glowered at him.

The telephone rang, and Waid said, "I'll answer it."

Mason turned to Charles Sabin and said significantly, "I have recently come into the possession of certain information, Mr. Sabin, which leads me to believe that your father had every reason to believe that by Monday, the fifth of this month, Mrs. Sabin would have obtained a divorce. I can't interpret the information I have received in any other light."

"That's a defamation of character," Mrs. Sabin said belligerently.

Mason kept his eyes on Charles Sabin. "Do you," he asked, "know anything about that?"

Sabin shook his head.

Mason turned back to Mrs. Sabin. "When were you in Paris, Mrs. Sabin?"

"That's none of your business."

"Did you get a divorce while you were in Paris?"

"Most certainly not!"

"Because," Mason went on, "if you did, I'll find out about it sooner or later, and I'm warning you now that I'm going to look for evidence that will . . ."

"Bosh," she said.

Richard Waid, who had been standing in the door near the hallway in which the telephone was located, came striding into the room and said, "Well, it isn't bosh, it's absolute fact."

"What do you know about it?" Mason asked.

Waid came into the room, met Mrs. Sabin's eyes, and turned to Charles Sabin. "I know everything about it. Look here, Mr. Sabin, I realize there's going to be a family fight. I know enough of Mrs. Sabin's character to know that it's going to be a free-for-all. As she pointed out to me, within a few minutes after she arrived, I can best safeguard my interests by keeping my mouth shut and keeping out of it. But my conscience won't let me do that."

"You and your conscience," Mrs. Sabin said, her voice rising shrilly. "You're nothing but a paid 'yesman.' My husband had completely lost confidence in you. You may not know it, but he was getting ready to discharge you. He . . ."

"Mrs. Sabin," Waid interrupted, "didn't go around the world, at all."

"She didn't?" Mason asked.

"No," Waid said, "that was just a stall to fool the newspaper reporters so she could get a divorce without any publicity. She boarded a round-the-world boat. She only went as far as Honolulu. Then she took the Clipper back, and established a residence at Reno. She obtained a divorce there. All this was done under Mr. Sabin's direction. She was to receive one hundred thousand dollars in cash when she furnished Mr. Sabin with evidence that she had received her divorce. Then she was to fly to New York, pick up a round-the-world boat, come back through the Panama Canal, and then let Mr. Sabin, at such time as he thought best, announce the divorce. That was the agreement between them."

Mrs. Sabin said with cold finality, "Richard, I warned you to keep your mouth shut about that."

Waid said, "I didn't tell the sheriff because I felt it wasn't up to me to discuss Mr. Sabin's business. I didn't tell Mr. Charles Sabin because Mrs. Sabin told me that it would be to my own good to keep my mouth shut. She said that if I co-operated with her, she'd co-operate with me once she got in the saddle."

"The question," Mason said, "is whether this divorce was actually obtained."

Mrs. Sabin settled back in her chair. "Very well," she said to Richard Waid. "This is your party. Go ahead and furnish the entertainment."

Waid said, "I will. The facts in this case are bound to come out sooner or later, anyway. Fremont C. Sabin had been unhappy for some time. He and his wife had been virtually separated. He wanted his freedom; his wife wanted a cash settlement.

"For some reason, Mr. Sabin wanted to have the matter remain a closely guarded secret. He didn't trust any of his regular attorneys with the matter, but went to a man by the name of C. William Desmond. I don't know whether any of you gentlemen know him."

"I know of him," Mason said, "a very reputable attorney. Go ahead, Waid. Tell me what happened."

Waid said, "An agreement was reached by which Mrs. Sabin agreed to get a divorce in Reno. When she presented a certified copy of the divorce decree to Mr. Sabin, he was to pay her the sum of one hundred thousand dollars in cash. It was stipulated as part of the agreement that there was to be absolutely no publicity, and that the responsibility was up to Mrs. Sabin to arrange the matter in such a way that the newspapers would not get hold of it."

"Then she didn't go around the world, after all?" Mason asked.

"No, of course not. As I told you, she went only as far as Honolulu, took the Clipper ship back, established a six weeks' residence in Reno, secured a decree of divorce, and went to New York. That was what Mr. Sabin telephoned to me about on the evening of the fifth. He said that everything was arranged and Mrs. Sabin was to meet me in New York with the decree of divorce. As I've already explained to the officers, Steve was waiting at the airport with his plane all tuned up and ready. I stepped in and we took off for New York. We arrived in New York on the afternoon of the sixth. I went directly to the bankers to whom Mr. Sabin had directed me, and also to the firm of solicitors who represented Mr. Sabin in New York. I wanted them to check over the certified decree of divorce before I paid over the money."

"They did so?" Mason asked.

"Yes."

"And when did you pay the money?"

"I paid that on the evening of Wednesday, the seventh, at a New York hotel."

"How was it paid?"

"In cash."

"Certified check or currency or . . ."

"Cash," Waid said. "It was paid in one hundred bills of one thousand dollars each. That was the way Mrs. Sabin wanted it."

"You have a receipt from her?" Mason asked.

"Yes, of course."

"And how about the certified copy of the decree of divorce?"

"I have that."

"Why," Charles Sabin asked, "didn't you tell me about this before, Richard?"

"I wanted to wait until Mr. Mason was here."

Mason turned to Mrs. Sabin. "How about it, Mrs. Sabin? Is this correct?" he asked.

"This is Waid's party," she said. "Let him go ahead

with the entertainment. He's played his first number, now let's have an encore."

"Fortunately," Waid said, "I insisted on the money being paid in the presence of witnesses. I thought that perhaps she was getting ready to pull one of her fast ones."

"Let's see the certified copy of the decree of divorce," Mason said.

Waid took from his pocket a folded paper.

"You should have delivered this to *me*," Charles Sabin said.

"I'm sorry," Waid apologized, "but Mr. Sabin's instructions were that I was to keep the decree of divorce and deliver it to no one except himself. I was not, under any circumstances, to mention it to anyone. The nature of the business which took me to New York was to be so confidential that no one, save his New York counselors, was to know anything about it. He particularly cautioned me against saying anything to you. I realize now, of course, that the situation is changed. Either you or Mrs. Sabin is going to be in charge of the entire estate, and my employment—if it continues—is going to be subject to your instructions.

"Mrs. Sabin has taken particular pains to tell me that she's going to be in the saddle and that if I say anything to anybody, I'll suffer for it."

Mason reached out and took the folded paper from Waid's hand. Sabin crossed over to look over the lawyer's shoulder.

"This," Mason said, as he examined the printed form with the certification attached to it, "appears to be in proper form."

"It was passed on by the New York lawyers," Waid said.

Mrs. Sabin chuckled.

Sabin said, "In that event this woman isn't my father's widow. As I take it, Mr. Mason, under those circumstances she isn't entitled to share in any part of the estate—that is, unless there's a specific devise or bequest in a will."

Mrs. Sabin's chuckle became harsh, mocking laughter.

"Your lawyer isn't saying anything," she said. "You over-played your hand, Charles; you killed him too soon."

"*I* killed him!" Charles Sabin exclaimed.

"You heard what I said."

"Moms," Steve Watkins pleaded, "please be careful of what you say."

"I'm more than careful," she said, "I'm truthful. Go ahead, Mr. Mason, why don't you tell them the bad news."

Mason glanced up to confront Sabin's troubled eyes.

"What's the matter?" Charles Sabin asked. "Isn't the decree good?"

Waid said, "It has to be good. The New York lawyers passed on it. A hundred thousand dollars was paid on the strength of that decree."

Mason said quietly, "You'll notice, gentlemen, that the decree of divorce was granted on Tuesday the sixth. There's nothing on here to show at what time on the sixth the decree was rendered."

"What does that have to do with it?" Sabin asked.

"Simply this," Mason said. "If Fremont C. Sabin was killed *before* Mrs. Sabin was divorced, the divorce was inoperative. She became his widow immediately upon his death. You can't get a divorce from a dead man."

And the silence which followed was broken by Mrs. Sabin's shrill laughter. "I tell you, Charles, you killed him too soon."

Slowly, Charles Sabin crossed the room to sit down in his chair.

"But," Mason went on, "in the event your father was killed *after* the divorce decree was granted, the situation is different."

"He was killed in the morning," Mrs. Sabin said positively, "after he'd returned from a fishing trip. Richard Waid has gone over all the facts with me in a preliminary conference. Those facts can't be changed and can't be distorted . . . because I'm going to see to it that no one changes them."

Mason said, "There are several factors involved in fixing the time, Mrs. Sabin."

"And that," she said, "is where I come in. I'm going to

see that none of the evidence is tampered with. My husband met his death before noon on the sixth. I didn't get my divorce until four-thirty in the afternoon."

"Of course, the decree of divorce doesn't show at what time during the day the decree was granted," Mason said.

"Well, I guess my testimony amounts to something, doesn't it?" she snapped. "I know when I got the divorce. What's more, I'll get a letter from the lawyer who represented me in Reno."

Charles Sabin looked at Mason with worried eyes. "The evidence," he said, "shows my father met his death some time before noon, probably around eleven o'clock."

Mrs. Sabin said nothing, but rocked back and forth, triumphantly, in the big rocking chair.

Charles Sabin turned to her savagely. "You have been rather free with your accusations directed at me," he said, "but what were *you* doing about that time? If anyone had a motive for killing him, you did."

Her smile was expansive. "Don't let your anger get the best of you, Charles," she said. "It's bad for your blood pressure. You know what the doctor told you. . . . You see, Charles, I was in Reno getting my divorce. Court was called at two o'clock, and I had to wait two hours and a half before my case came up. I'm afraid you'll have to find a pretty big loophole in that alibi to pin the crime on me—or don't you think so?"

Mason said, "I'm going to tell you something which hasn't as yet been made public. The authorities at San Molinas will probably discover it shortly. In the meantime, the facts happen to be in my possession. I think you all should know them."

"I don't care what facts you have," Mrs. Sabin said. "You're not going to bluff me."

"I'm not bluffing anybody," Mason told her. "Fremont C. Sabin crossed over into Mexico and went through a marriage ceremony with a librarian from San Molinas. Her name is Helen Monteith. It has generally been supposed that the parrot which was found in the cabin, with the body, was Casanova, the parrot to which Mr. Sabin

67

was very much attached. As a matter of fact, for reasons which I haven't been able to uncover as yet, Mr. Sabin purchased another parrot in San Molinas and left Casanova with Helen Monteith. Casanova remained with Helen Monteith from Friday, the second, until today."

Mrs. Sabin got to her feet. "Well," she said, "I don't see that this concerns *me*, and I don't think we have anything further to gain here. You, Richard Waid, are going to be sorry that you betrayed my interests and violated my instructions. I suppose now I've got to go to a lot of trouble making affidavits as to when that divorce decree was actually granted. . . . So my husband has a bigamous wife, has he? Well, well, well! Come, Steve, we'll go and leave these gentlemen to themselves. As soon as I've gone, they'll try to find evidence which will show that Fremont wasn't killed until the evening of Tuesday the sixth. In order to do that, it's quite possible they'll try to tamper with the evidence. I think, Steve, that it will be wise for us to retain a lawyer. We have our own interests to protect."

She swept from the room. Steve Watkins, following her, turned to make some fumbling attempt to comply with conventions. "Pleased to have met you, Mr. Mason," he said, and to Charles Sabin, "You understand how things are with me, Uncle Charles."

When they had left the room, Charles Sabin said, "I think that woman has the most irritating personality of any woman I have ever encountered. How about it, Mr. Mason? Do I have to sit quietly by and let her accuse me of murdering my father?"

"What would you *like* to do?" Mason asked.

"I'd like to tell her just what I think of her. I'd like to let her know that she isn't fooling me for a minute, that she's simply a shrewd, gold-digging, fortune-hunting . . ."

"That wouldn't do you any good," Mason interrupted. "You'd tell her what you thought of her. She'd tell you what she thought of you. I take it, Mr. Sabin, you haven't had a great deal of experience in giving people what is colloquially known as a piece of your mind, have you?"

"No, sir," Sabin admitted.

Mason said, "Well, she evidently has. When it comes to

an exchange of personal vituperation, she'd quite probably have you beaten before you started. If you want to fight her, there's only one way to fight."

"What's that?" Sabin asked, his voice showing his interest.

"That is to hit her where she least expects to be hit. There's only one way to fight, and that's to win. Never attack *where* the other man is expecting it, *when* the other man is expecting it. That's where he's prepared his strongest defense."

"Well," Sabin demanded, "where can we attack her where she hasn't her defenses organized?"

"That," Mason said, "remains to be seen."

"Why," Sabin asked, "should my father have gone to all these elaborate preparations to insure secrecy about that divorce? I can understand, of course, that my father didn't like publicity. He wanted to avoid all publicity as much as possible. Some things are inevitable. When a man gets divorced, it's necessary for the world to know he's divorced."

"I think," Mason said, "that your father probably had some reasons for wanting to keep his picture out of the newspaper at that particular time, although it's rather hard to tell."

Sabin thought for a moment. "You mean that he was already courting this other girl, and didn't want her to know who he was?"

Richard Waid said, "If you'll pardon me, I think I can clear that situation up. I happen to know that Fremont C. Sabin was rather . . . er . . . gun-shy about women, after his experience with the present Mrs. Sabin . . . Well, I feel quite certain that if he had wanted to marry again, he would have taken every possible precaution to see that he wasn't getting a gold-digger."

Charles Sabin frowned. "The thing," he said, "gets more and more complicated. Of course, my father had a horror of publicity. I gather that the plans for this divorce were made before he met this young woman in San Molinas, but probably he was just trying to avoid reporters. What's all this about the parrot, Mr. Mason?"

"You mean Casanova?"

"Yes."

"Apparently," Mason said, "for reasons best known to himself, your father decided to put Casanova in a safe place for a while, and take another parrot with him to the mountain cabin."

"Good heavens, why?" Sabin asked. "The *parrot* wasn't in any danger, was he?"

Mason shrugged his shoulders and said, "We haven't all the facts available as yet."

"If you'll permit me to make a suggestion," Waid said, "it seems that the parrot most decidedly was *not* in any danger. The person who murdered Mr. Sabin was especially solicitous about the welfare of the parrot."

Mason said, *"Peculiarly* solicitous, would be a better word, Waid . . . Well, I must be going. I have quite a few irons in the fire. You'll hear from me later on."

Sabin followed him to the door. "I'm particularly anxious to have this cleared up, Mr. Mason."

Mason grinned. "So am I," he said. "I'll have photostatic copies made of this divorce decree and then we'll chase down the court records."

CHAPTER SIX

MASON was two blocks from the office building which contained his office and that of the Drake Detective Agency, when his car was suddenly enveloped in the red glare of a police spotlight. A siren screamed him over to the curb.

Mason stopped his car and frowned across at the police automobile being driven by Sergeant Holcomb. "Well," he asked, "what's the excitement?"

Holcomb said, "A couple of gentlemen want to talk with you, Mason."

Sheriff Barnes opened the door in the rear of the car, and was followed by a closely coupled man, some ten years younger, who pushed his way across to Mason's car, and instantly assumed the conversational lead. "You're Mason?" he demanded.

Mason nodded.

"I'm Raymond Sprague, the district attorney from San Molinas."

"Glad to know you," Mason told him.

"We want to talk with you."

"What about?" Mason asked.

"About Helen Monteith."

"What about her?" Mason inquired.

"Where is she?"

"I don't know," Mason told him.

Sheriff Barnes said, "We'd better go some place where we can talk it over."

"My office is within a couple of blocks," Mason pointed out.

"And the Drake Detective Agency is in the same building, isn't it?" Sprague inquired.

"Yes."

"You were on your way there?" Sprague asked.

"Does it," Mason inquired, "make any particular difference?"

"I think it does," Sprague told him.

"Well, of course," Mason remarked, "I have no means of knowing just what you have in mind."

"That isn't answering my question," Sprague said.

"Were you asking a question?"

Sheriff Barnes interposed. "Now, wait a minute, Ray," he said. "That's not getting us anywhere," and, with a significant glance toward the curious pedestrians, who had gathered on the sidewalk, "It isn't doing the case any good. Let's go up to Mason's office."

Mason kicked out the clutch and snapped the car into low gear. "I'll see you there," he said.

The others jumped into the police car, followed closely behind, until Mason had parked his machine. They rode up in the elevator with him and entered his private office. When Mason had switched on the lights and closed the door, Sergeant Holcomb said, "Don't say I didn't warn you birds about this guy."

"You didn't warn me," Raymond Sprague said, "you warned the sheriff."

"Just what," Mason asked, "is the beef about?"

"What have you done with Helen Monteith?"

"Nothing," Mason said.

"We think differently," Sprague announced.

"Suppose you tell me what you think," Mason said.

"You've had Helen Monteith take a powder."

Mason faced them, his feet spread far apart, his shoulders squared, his hands thrust into the side pockets of his coat. "All right," he said, "let's get this straight. I'm representing Helen Monteith. I'm also representing Charles Sabin. I'm trying to solve the murder of Fremont C. Sabin. I'm being paid money by my clients for doing just that. You gentlemen are being paid money by your county for solving the same murder I'm trying to solve. Naturally, you're going to solve it your way, and, by the same token, I intend to solve it mine."

"We want to question Helen Monteith," Sprague said.

Mason met his eyes squarely. "Go ahead and question her, then."

"Where is she?"

Mason pulled his cigarette case from his pocket and said, "I've told you once I don't know. You're running this show, I'm not."

"You wouldn't want me to charge you with being an accessory after the fact, would you?" Sprague asked ominously.

"I don't give a damn what you charge me with," Mason told him. "Only, if you want to talk law, remember that I can't be an accessory after the fact, unless I give aid to the murderer. Now then, do you intend to claim that Helen Monteith is the one who committed the murder?"

Sprague flushed and said, "Yes."

Sheriff Barnes interposed a drawling comment. "Now wait a minute, Ray, let's not get our cart before our horse."

"I know what I'm doing," Sprague said.

Mason turned to Sheriff Barnes and said, "I think you and I can get along, Sheriff."

"I'm not so certain," Barnes said, pulling a sack of tobacco from his pocket, and spilling rattling grains to the surface of a brown cigarette paper. "You have quite a bit to explain before I'll give you my confidence again."

"What, for instance?" Mason asked.

"I thought you were going to co-operate with me."

"I am," Mason told him, "to the extent that I intend to find out who murdered Fremont C. Sabin."

"We want to find out, too."

"I know you do. You use your methods. I'll use mine."

"We don't like having those methods interfered with."

"I can understand that," Mason told him.

Sprague said, "Don't waste words talking with him."

"If you birds want to charge him with compounding a felony, or being an accessory after the fact," Sergeant Holcomb said, "I'll take him into custody with the greatest of pleasure."

Mason struck a match and held it to Sheriff Barnes' cigarette, then lit his own. The conversation came to an abrupt standstill. After a few moments Mason said to Sprague, "Are you going to take him up on that, Sprague?"

"I think I am," Sprague snapped, "but I'm going to get some evidence first."

"I don't think you'll find much here in my office," Mason pointed out.

Holcomb said, "I'll take him down to headquarters, if you fellows say the word."

Sheriff Barnes turned to face them. "Now listen," he said, "you boys have been kicking me around because I gave Mason a break. I still don't see any reason why we should be stampeded into going off half cocked. Personally, I'm not going to get antagonistic until I find out a few things." He turned to Mason and said, "Did you know that the gun which killed Fremont C. Sabin was taken from a collection at the public library in San Molinas?"

"What if it was?" Mason asked.

"And the librarian, Helen Monteith, went through a marriage ceremony with a man who gave the name of George Wallman, and whom neighbors identify absolutely as being Fremont C. Sabin?"

"Go ahead," Sergeant Holcomb said sarcastically, "give him all the information you have, and when he gets done he'll laugh at you."

"On the contrary," Mason said, "I'm very much inclined to co-operate. Having gone that far, I presume you gentlemen have noticed that the caged parrot on the screen porch of Helen Monteith's little bungalow is Casanova, the parrot owned by Fremont C. Sabin, and that the parrot which was found in the mountain cabin is a parrot which Sabin had recently purchased from the Fifth Avenue Pet Shop in San Molinas?"

Sheriff Barnes' eyes widened for a moment, then narrowed. "You're giving us the straight goods on that?" he asked.

"Absolutely," Mason said.

"He's drawing a red herring across the trail," Sergeant Holcomb said disgustedly.

"If you knew all of that," Raymond Sprague said, "and *then* hid Helen Monteith where we couldn't question her, I think I *will* charge you with being an accessory."

"Go ahead," Mason invited. "As I remember the law, you'll have to charge that I concealed a principal in a felony case, with the intent that such principal might avoid or escape from arrest, trial, conviction or punishment, having knowledge that said principal had committed such felony, or had been charged with such felony. Now then, as I gather it, to date Helen Monteith hasn't been charged with the commission of any felony."

"No, she hasn't," Barnes admitted.

"And *I* don't think she has committed any felony," Mason said.

"Well, I do," Sprague told him.

"A mere difference of opinion," Mason observed; and then turned once more to Sheriff Barnes. "It may interest you to know, Sheriff," he said, "that the parrot in the cage on Helen Monteith's porch keeps saying, 'Put down that gun, Helen . . . don't shoot . . . My God, you've shot me.' "

The sheriff's face showed his interest. "How do you account for that?" he asked.

"I don't," Mason said. "Of course, the obvious way to account for it is that the parrot was present when someone named Helen threatened someone with a gun, and then, after being told to drop the gun, fired a shot, which took effect. However, the shooting took place, not in Helen Monteith's bungalow, but in a mountain cabin some miles away, while, apparently, the parrot on Helen Monteith's porch wasn't present at the shooting."

"Just what are you getting at?" Sheriff Barnes inquired.

"I'm trying to co-operate with you," Mason told him.

"Well, we don't want your co-operation," Sprague told him. "It's quite evident to me that you've gathered a great deal of information from questioning Helen Monteith. Now, I'm going to give you twenty-four hours to produce her. In the event you fail to do so, I'm going to have you brought before the Grand Jury at San Molinas."

"Better make it twelve hours," Sergeant Holcomb suggested.

Sprague hesitated a moment, then looked at his watch and said, "You have her in San Molinas for questioning before the Grand Jury by noon tomorrow. Otherwise, you'll take the consequences."

He nodded to Sergeant Holcomb, and they started for the door. Mason caught Sheriff Barnes' eye and said, "Going, Sheriff, or do *you* want to stay?"

Sheriff Barnes dropped easily into the overstuffed leather chair and said, "Don't go just yet, Ray."

"We're not getting anywhere here," Sprague objected.

"I am," the sheriff said, puffing calmly at his cigarette.

Mason seated himself on one corner of his big office desk. Sprague hesitated a moment, then walked across to a chair. Sergeant Holcomb, making no attempt to conceal his disgust, stood by the door leading to the corridor.

Mason said to Sheriff Barnes, "Rather a peculiar situation developed out at Sabin's house. It seems that Mrs.

Sabin and Fremont C. Sabin entered into an agreement by which she was to pretend to take a round-the-world trip, double back by Clipper ship to the coast, go to Reno, establish a residence, and get a divorce, taking pains to avoid any publicity whatsoever. Having done that, she was to receive, in full payment of any claims she might have as the wife of Fremont C. Sabin, the sum of one hundred thousand dollars in cash."

"She wasn't in Reno. She was on a boat coming through the Panama Canal, when we located her," Sprague said. "That Reno business is some sort of a pipe dream."

"Perhaps it is," Mason admitted, "but Richard Waid met her in New York on Wednesday the seventh. She gave him a certified copy of a decree of divorce, and he gave her one hundred thousand dollars, and holds her receipt for it. That's the important business which took him to New York."

"What are you getting at, Mason?" Sheriff Barnes asked.

"Simply this," Mason said. "The decree was dated on Tuesday the sixth. If a divorce decree was granted *before* Sabin was murdered, his widow received one hundred thousand dollars after his death, in accordance with an agreement which had been entered into. But, if Sabin was murdered *before* the divorce decree was granted, then the divorce decree was invalid, Mrs. Sabin has received one hundred thousand dollars in cash, and is also entitled to take a share of the estate as the surviving widow of the decedent. That's rather an interesting, and somewhat complicated, legal point, gentlemen."

Sergeant Holcomb said wearily, "Listen. Helen Monteith married Sabin. She didn't know he was married. She thought his name was Wallman, but she went up to that cabin with him. We traced those clothes through the laundry mark. They were hers. She'd found out he was married. She figured he'd been taking her for a ride. She made up her mind she was going to call for a showdown. She wanted a gun, and she wanted one right away. She couldn't get into a store to get a gun, but there was a collection of weapons in the library. She had a key to that collection. She picked out a gun, intending to return it to the collection. Perhaps she only wanted to run a bluff, I don't know. Perhaps it was self-defense. I don't know and I don't care. But she took that gun up to the cabin and killed Fremont C. Sabin.

"She ran to Mason to represent her. He's found out stuff which he could only have found out after having talked with her. She told her sister she was going to Sabin's residence and talk with the son. Apparently, she never showed up at the residence. Mason was there. He went out there with his secretary. He comes back alone. Where's his secretary? Where's Helen Monteith?

"You start questioning him, and he starts drawing Mrs. Sabin across the trail as a red herring. He'll get you more red herrings as fast as you fall for them."

A peculiar knock sounded on the corridor door. Mason slid to his feet, walked across the office, and opened the door. Paul Drake, on the threshold, said, "Well, Perry, I've . . ." and broke off as he saw the people gathered in the room.

"Come in, Paul," Mason said. "You know Sergeant Holcomb, of course, and this is Sheriff Barnes of San Molinas, and Raymond Sprague, the district attorney of San Molinas. What have you found out?"

"Do you," Drake asked, "want me to report here?"

"Sure," Mason told him.

"Well, I've been burning up the long distance telephone and getting operatives on the job. As nearly as I can tell right now, Mrs. Sabin sailed to Honolulu, took the Clipper ship back from Honolulu, went to Reno, and stayed at the Silver City Bungalows, establishing a residence under the name of Helen W. Sabin. At the end of six weeks she probably filed suit for divorce against Fremont C. Sabin, but I can't get into the courthouse records until tomorrow morning. On the evening of Wednesday the seventh, Mrs. Sabin was in New York. She sailed from New York at midnight."

"Then she was in Reno until when?" Mason asked of the detective.

"As nearly as we can find out, she took the plane from

Reno on the evening of Tuesday the sixth and arrived in New York on the seventh."

"Then the divorce decree must have been granted the morning of the sixth," Raymond Sprague said.

"It would look that way," Drake told him.

Sprague nodded and said, "She must have been in court on the sixth."

"What are you getting at?" Sheriff Barnes inquired.

"I'm just checking up," Sprague told him. "Mason has defeated his own purpose."

"How do you mean?" Barnes asked.

"Simply this," Sprague said. "Mason's trying to distract our attention from Helen Monteith by dangling Mrs. Sabin in front of our noses, but if she was in court in Reno, she could hardly have been killing her husband in a mountain cabin in San Molinas County at one and the same time. Regardless of what other things the woman may have done, she couldn't have been concerned in the murder."

Mason stretched his arms above his head and sucked in a prodigious yawn. "Well, gentlemen," he observed, "at least *I'm* putting *my* cards on the table."

Raymond Sprague walked across to the door. "I think," he said, "we're fully capable of making our own investigations. As far as you're concerned, Mason, you heard my ultimatum. You either have Helen Monteith before the Grand Jury at San Molinas at twelve o'clock tomorrow, or *you'll* go before the Grand Jury."

Sheriff Barnes was the last to leave the office. He seemed reluctant to go. In the corridor he said in an undertone, "Aren't you acting a bit hasty, Ray?"

The district attorney's answer was a rumbling undertone, drowned by the slamming of the door.

Mason grinned at Paul Drake and said, "Well, Paul, that's that."

"Are you keeping Helen Monteith out of sight somewhere?" Drake asked.

Mason smiled at him and said, "I don't have the slightest idea, Paul, where Helen Monteith is."

"My man reported that you picked her up out at Sabin's residence, and that she and Della Street drove off in her car."

Mason said, "I trust the man who made that report to you won't do any talking to outsiders, Paul."

"He won't," Drake said. "What are you going to do about having her before the Grand Jury in San Molinas, Perry?"

"I can't get her there," Mason said. "I don't know where she is."

"Della does."

"I don't know were Della is."

"Well," Drake told him, "it's your funeral."

"How about that wire tapping?" Mason asked. "What have you found out about it?"

"Not a darned thing," Drake confessed. "And the more I dig into it, the less I know."

"Some of the gambling element," Mason asked, "wanting to get a line on what's happening in this vice crusade?"

"Not a chance," Drake told him.

"Why not?"

"The gamblers aren't worried."

"Why?"

"Because they aren't. They're too strongly entrenched."

"That Citizens' Committee was digging up a lot of evidence," Mason said.

"Not evidence that would convict anybody of anything. Just evidence that gives rise to a lot of suspicion. Gamblers, and all forms of organized vice, figure on that stuff, Perry. Every so often there's a clean-up and a shakedown. Some of the small fry try to fight back. They struggle against the stream. The big fish don't; they just drift along with the current and wait for the police to clear things up."

"The police?" Mason asked.

"Sure," Drake said. "Figure this, Perry. Whenever there's a recognized vice district, or open gambling, there's police graft. That doesn't mean all of the policemen are in on it. It means *some* of the policemen are, and it means some of the higher-ups are. Whenever there's a squawk, the big shots in the vice game simply sit back and say to their cronies on the police force, 'Okay, you birds tell us when it's safe to open up again. In the meantime, we're both losing income, so you'd better hurry.' "

"Then you don't think the big-shot gamblers were trying to listen in on Sabin's telephone conversations?"

"Not one chance in a hundred. They just pulled in their horns and took a vacation . . . To tell you the truth, Perry, it looks more like a private job to me."

"You mean private detectives?"

"Yes."

"Employed by whom?" Mason asked.

"Mrs. Sabin, on a hunch," Drake told him. "Taken by and large, Perry, that woman doesn't seem to me to be exactly dumb."

"No," Mason admitted, "her mother didn't raise many foolish children . . . You have your car, Paul?"

"Yes. Why?"

"I have a job for you."

"What is it?"

"You're going with me," Mason told him, "and we're making a rush trip to San Molinas."

"What for?" Drake wanted to know.

"We're going to steal a parrot," Mason said.

"Steal a parrot?"

"That's what I said."

"You mean Casanova?"

"Yes."

"What the devil do you want with *him?*"

Mason said, "Get right down to brass tacks, Paul, and what do you have? You have a case which entirely revolves around a parrot. Casanova is the key clew to the whole affair. Notice that whoever killed Sabin was particularly solicitous about the welfare of the parrot."

"You mean that it was someone who loved the parrot, or was tender-hearted about birds in general?"

Mason said, "I don't know yet exactly *what* the reason was. However, I'm commencing to have an idea. Notice, moreover, Paul, that lately Casanova says, 'Put down that gun, Helen . . . don't shoot . . . My God, you've shot me.' "

"Meaning that Casanova must have been the parrot

which was present when the shots were fired?" Drake asked. "And that whoever committed the murder took Casanova away, and subsequently substituted another parrot?"

"Why," Mason asked, "would a murderer do that?"

"To tell you the truth, Perry, I don't know. That parrot angle sounds goofy to me."

"Well," Mason said, "any explanation which has been offered to me so far sounds goofy; but my best hunch is that that parrot offers the key to the situation. Now, Helen Monteith isn't home. The sheriff and the district attorney of San Molinas County are wandering around here trying to chase down developments at this end, with the help of Sergeant Holcomb. It *should* be an excellent time to raid San Molinas."

"If they catch you cutting corners in that county, you're going to jail," Drake warned.

"I know it," Mason admitted, grinning, "and that's why I don't want to be caught cutting corners. If you have your car here, let's go."

"You going to lift cage and all?" Drake asked.

"Uh-huh," Mason said, "and I'm going to put another parrot in place of the one that's there."

He picked up his telephone, dialed a number, and after a moment said, "Hello, Helmold, this is Perry Mason, the lawyer. I'd like to get you to run down to your pet store and open the place up. I want to buy a parrot."

CHAPTER SEVEN

THE parrot, in the back of the car, squawked from time to time slumberous noises of parrot protest as the lurching of the car forced him to fight for his balance.

Drake, at the wheel, seemed particularly pessimistic as to the probable outcome of their mission, while Mason, settled comfortably back against the cushions, smoked cigarettes and stared in meditative silence at the unwinding ribbon of moonlit road which flashed past beneath the headlights of the speeding car.

"Don't overlook the fact that Reno isn't so very far away—not by airplane," Drake said. "If Mrs. Sabin was in Reno, and *if* she was the one who employed private detectives to tap Sabin's telephone line, then you'd better forget this Monteith woman."

"How much do you charge for tapping telephone wires?" Mason asked.

Drake was sufficiently startled to take his eyes momentarily from the road. *"Me?"* he asked.

"Uh-huh."

Drake said, "Listen, Perry, I'll do darn near anything for you, but tapping a telephone line is a felony in this state. I'm certainly not going to do *that* for you."

"That's what I figured," Mason observed.

"What're you getting at?" Drake wanted to know.

"Simply this, Paul; those telephone lines were tapped. *You* don't think the gamblers did it. It doesn't look as though the police did it. You think a private detective agency did it. It's my guess a detective agency would think twice before it went in for wire-tapping."

"Some of 'em would," Drake said, "some of 'em wouldn't. There are some chaps in this game who would do anything for money. However, I get your point, Perry, and you *may* be right. Remember this, that most of the wire-tapping these days is done by the police."

"Why the police?" Mason asked.

"Oh, I don't know. Of course, they figure that laws don't apply to them. You'd be surprised to know how extensively they do tap telephone lines and listen in on conversations. It's almost a matter of investigative routine."

"Well, it's an interesting subject for speculation," Mason agreed. "If the telephone lines were tapped by the police, Sergeant Holcomb must have known about it. And if that's the case, the police must have records of the conversations which took place over that telephone . . . You check up on those divorce records first thing in the morning, Paul."

"I'm going to," Drake said. "I have two men waiting in

Reno. They're going through the records just as soon as they become available."

They drove for several miles in thoughtful silence, until a sign announced the city limits of San Molinas.

"Want to go directly to Helen Monteith's house?" Drake asked.

"Make certain we're not being followed," Mason said, sliding around in the seat so he could look through the back window.

"I've been checking pretty carefully on that," Drake told him.

"Well, make a figure eight, just for the sake of being absolutely certain," Mason said.

When Drake had completed the maneuver, Mason nodded his satisfaction. "Okay, Paul, drive right to the bungalow."

"That's rather a snoopy neighbor," Drake observed thoughtfully. "We'd better switch out the lights a block or so before we get to the house . . . How about parking a few doors away, Perry?"

"No," Mason said, "I want to make it fast. You can drive around the block once, and I'll size up the situation, then switch off your lights, and swing in to the curb as near the screen porch as you can make it . . . I hope this damned parrot doesn't squawk when I start moving him."

"I thought parrots slept at night," Drake said.

"They do," Mason told him. "But when they're being dragged around the country in automobiles, they get nervous—and I don't know how much of a squawk Casanova will make when I steal *him*."

Drake said, "Now listen, Perry, let's be reasonable about this thing. If anything goes wrong, don't get pigheaded and keep trying to make the switch. I'll be all ready to make a getaway. For God's sake, drop that parrot and make a run for it."

"I don't think anything will go wrong," Mason told him, "—not unless the house is being watched, and we should be able to find that out by swinging around the block."

"Well, we'll know in a minute," Drake said, turning the

wheel sharply to the left. "We're within two blocks of the place now."

He ran two blocks and swung once more to the left. Mason sized up the bungalow as they glided past. "The house is dark," he said. "There are lights in the house next door, and lights across the street. The screen porch looks easy."

Drake said, "Maybe you think it won't be a relief to me when this is over, Perry."

He circled the block, swung in to the curb, with lights out and motor off.

Mason glided out of the car, the cage and the parrot in his hand, and vanished into the shadows. He found it a simple matter to cut the screen, snap back the catch on the screen door and effect an entrance to the porch. The parrot he had brought with him was restive, moving about on the perch in the cage, but Casanova, apparently drugged with sleep, barely stirred when Mason gently lowered the cage from its hook, and substituted the cage he had brought with him.

A few moments later, Mason had deposited Casanova in the back of the automobile. "Okay, Paul," he said.

Drake needed no signal. He lurched the car into motion, just as the door of the adjoining house opened and the ample figure of Mrs. Winters stood framed in the doorway.

As Paul Drake skidded around the corner, with the lights out, the parrot in the back of the car mumbled sleepily, "My God, you've shot me."

CHAPTER EIGHT

MASON unlocked the door of his private office, and then suddenly stood motionless, staring in surprise at Della Street.

"You!" he exclaimed.

"None other," she told him, blinking back tears. "I guess you'll have to get a new secretary, Chief."

"What's the matter, Della?" he asked, coming toward her solicitously.

She started to cry then, and he slid his arm around her shoulders, patting her reassuringly. "What happened?" he asked.

"That t-t-t-two-timing little d-d-d-devil," she said.

"Who?" Mason asked.

"That librarian, Helen Monteith."

"What about her, Della?"

"She slipped one over on me."

"Come on over here; sit down and tell me about it," Mason said.

"Oh, Chief, I'm so d-d-darned sorry I let you down!"

"How do you figure you let me down, Della? Perhaps you didn't let me down as much as you think."

"Yes, I did too. You told me to keep her where no one could find her, and . . ."

"What happened?" Mason asked. "Did they find her, or did she take a run-out powder?"

"She took a p-p-p-powder."

"All right, how did it happen?"

Della Street dabbed at her eyes with a lace-bordered handkerchief. "Gosh, Chief, I hate to be a b-b-bawl-baby," she said. ". . . Believe it or not, this is the first tear I've shed. . . . I could have wrung her neck with my bare hands. . . . She started in and told me a story that tore my heart inside out."

"What was the story?" Mason asked, his face without expression.

"It was the story of her romance," Della said. "She told it. . . . Oh, Chief, you'd have to be a woman to understand. . . . It was all about her life. She'd been romantically inclined when she was young. There'd been a high school, puppy-love affair, which had been pretty serious with her. . . . But it hadn't been so serious with the boy . . . that is, it had at the time, Chief. I don't know if you can get the sketch, I can't tell it to you the way she told it to me.

"This boy was just an awfully nice boy. She made me see him just the way she saw him—a nice, clean, decent chap, with something of the mystic, or spiritual, in him . . . something that a woman really wants in every man she loves, and this was a real love affair.

"Then the boy went away to get a job, so he could make enough money to marry her, and she was all thrilled with pride. And then, after a few months, he came back, and . . ."

". . . And he was in love with someone else?" Mason asked as she hesitated.

"No, it wasn't that," Della said. "He was still in love with her, but he'd become sort of smart-alecky. He looked on her as something of a conquest. He wasn't in such a hurry to get married, and he'd been running around with a crowd of boys that thought it wasn't smart to have ideals. They had a sophisticated attitude, and . . . well, I'll never forget the way she described it. She said the acid of their pseudo-realism had eaten the gold off his character and left just the base metal beneath."

"So then what happened?" Mason asked.

"Then she naturally became bitter—toward men and toward love. At a time when most girls were seeing the world through rose-tinted spectacles, she was embittered and disillusioned. She didn't care too much for dances, and parties, and things, and gradually became more and more interested in books. She said she formed her friendships among books; that books didn't tease you along until they'd won your friendship, and then suddenly reverse themselves and slap you in the face.

"Along about that time, she acquired the reputation of being narrow-minded and strait-laced, and a poor sport. It started in with a few fellows whose vanity was insulted because she wouldn't drink bathtub gin, and neck. They advertised her as an awful pill, and gradually that reputation stuck to her. Remember, Chief, she was in a small town. It's pretty hard for people to really see each other in a small town. They only see the reputation which has been built up by a lot of word-of-mouth advertising."

"Was that the way she described it?" Mason asked.

Della Street nodded.

"All right, go ahead. Then what happened?"

"Then, when she'd just about given up any idea of

romance, along came Fremont Sabin. He was kindly and gentle, he wasn't greedy. He had a philosophy of life which saw the beautiful side of everything. In other words, Chief, as nearly as I can explain it, there was something of the idealism in this man that she had worshiped in this boy with whom she'd been in love. But, whereas the boy had the ideals of youth, and they weren't strongly enough entrenched in him to withstand the cynicism and cheap worldly wisdom of his associates, this man had battled his way through every disillusionment life had to offer, and won his idealism as an achievement, as an ultimate goal. His ideals stood for something—they were carefully thought out. They'd stood the test of time."

"I guess," Mason said thoughtfully, "Fremont C. Sabin was really a wonderful character."

"Apparently he was, Chief. Of course, he played an awful trick on her, but . . ."

"I'm not so certain he did," Mason said. "We can look at the thing from Sabin's viewpoint, and see just what he was trying to do. When you get the whole picture in its proper perspective, and in the light of some new evidence we've uncovered, it's quite consistent with his character."

"Can you tell me about this new evidence, Chief?"

"No, you tell me about Helen Monteith first."

"Well, this man started coming to the library. She knew him only as Wallman, a man who was out of work, a man who had no particular trade, and no particular cause to feel friendly toward the world; yet he did. He was interested in books on philosophy and social reform, and he was particularly interested in his fellowmen. He'd sit in the library, sometimes at night, apparently reading a book, but in reality studying the men who were seated around him. And then, whenever he had an opportunity, he'd get acquainted, in an unostentatious manner, and listen. He was always listening.

"Naturally, Helen Monteith, as a librarian, watched him and became interested in him. He started talking to her. Apparently, he had quite a knack of drawing people out, and he got her to tell him a great deal about herself before she realized how much she actually was telling him. And then she fell in love. Because the man was older than she, and because she hadn't been anticipating anything of the sort, romance sneaked up on her and caught her unaware. She was madly in love with him before she even realized she *was* in love. And then when she found out that he loved her . . . Well, Chief, as she told me about it, she said it felt as though her soul was singing all the time."

"She must have something of a gift for expression," Mason said, his eyes narrowing slightly.

"No, Chief, it wasn't an act she was putting on. She was absolutely sincere. She loves to talk about it, because it was such a beautiful thing with her. Despite the shock of the tragedy, and all the disillusionment which has come with finding out he was married, she's still happy and philosophical about it all. She feels that she finally found happiness in her life. The happiness didn't last, but she doesn't seem to feel bitter about that, but, instead, is grateful for the measure of happiness she did have. Of course, when she read the morning paper about the murder, about how Sabin would go around using an assumed name, studying people, browsing in libraries . . . Well, of course, that made her suspicious. Then she saw the photograph of this mountain cabin and recognized it. But she fought against her fears, trying to convince herself against her better judgment. . . . And then the afternoon paper carried the picture of Sabin, and her worst fears were confirmed."

"Then you don't think she killed him?" Mason asked.

"Absolutely not," she said. "She couldn't . . . Well . . ."

"Why the doubt?" Mason asked, as her voice trailed off into silence.

"Well," Della said, "there is this side to her character. If she had thought that he had been going to do something to hurt her . . . If she had thought that his ideals were going to . . . well, not exactly his ideals, either, Chief, but if she had thought that there was something about him which was counterfeit, I think she'd have killed him, in order to keep from discovering it, if you know what I mean."

"I think I do," Mason told her. "Go on, what happened?"

"Well, I took her to a little hotel. I went to some precautions to make certain we couldn't be traced by the police. I gathered that was what you wanted. I got some baggage out of my apartment, and we registered as two sisters from Topeka, Kansas. I asked the clerk a lot of questions that tourists would ordinarily ask, and I think I completely sold him on the idea.

"We had a corner room, in the back, with twin beds and a bath, and quietly, in such a manner that she wouldn't notice what I was doing, I locked the door from the inside and put the key in my purse.

"Well, we sat down and talked, and she told me all about her romance, and about everything which had happened. I guess we talked for three or four hours. I know it was long after midnight when we went to bed; and I guess it was about five o'clock this morning when she woke me up, shaking me and telling me she couldn't get the door open. She was fully dressed, and seemed very much upset.

"I asked her why she wanted to get the door open, and she said she had to go back to San Molinas, that she simply *had* to. There was something she'd forgotten.

"I told her she couldn't go back. She said she must, and we had quite an argument. Finally, she said she was going to telephone the hotel and have someone come up to open the door. Then I got hard with her."

"What did you tell her?" Mason asked.

"I told her that you were sacrificing a great deal to help her, and that she was giving you a double-cross; that she was in danger, and that the police would catch her and charge her with murder; that her romance would be written up by every sob sister in the tabloid newspaper game; that she'd be dragged through courts, and the pitiless white light of searching and unfavorable publicity would beat upon her. . . . I told her everything I could think of. I talked like a lawyer working on a jury."

"What happened?"

"She still wanted to go," Della Street said; "so then I told her that the minute she walked out of that door, you were finished with her, you wouldn't protect her in any way; that she was going to have to obey your orders, and stay there, until I could get in touch with you. She wanted to know when I could get in touch with you, and I told her I didn't know, not until after you got to the office at around nine-thirty; that I could get Paul Drake to give you a message. She wanted me to call your apartment directly, and I told her absolutely nothing doing, because I was afraid the police would be plugged in on your line, and because I thought you didn't want to know where she was, or have anything to do with her disappearance.

"Well, she thought that over for a while and decided it was reasonable. She said that was all right, she'd wait until nine-thirty, but made me promise, solemnly, that I'd try and get in touch with you then. She undressed and went back to bed, and said she was sorry she'd made such a scene. It took me about half an hour to get composed enough to drop off to sleep again. . . . And I woke up, and she was gone. . . . She'd deliberately planned that business about giving in just so she could double-cross me."

"She'd taken the key out of your purse?" Mason asked.

"Of course not," Della Street said. "I had that purse tucked under my pillow slip. She couldn't have possibly got that key without waking me up. She went down the fire escape. The window was open."

"You don't know what time she went?" Mason asked.

"No."

"What time did you wake up?"

"Not until after eight o'clock," she said. "I was pretty tired, and I figured we wouldn't have anything to do except be waiting, so I sort of set my mental alarm clock for around eight o'clock. I woke up and lay there for a while, thinking she was over on the other bed, and being grateful that she'd calmed down. I slipped out quietly from between the covers, so as not to awaken her, and started to tiptoe to the bathroom, and then looked over my shoulder, and saw that her bed looked rather strange. I went over for another look. She'd pulled the old stunt of wadding up some blankets and a pillow, and putting them under the covers, to make it look as though someone was asleep in the bed. . . . Well, Chief, that's all there is to it."

Mason held her close to him. "Don't worry, Della," he said. "You certainly did all anyone could have done. . . . Where did she go, do you know?"

"I think she was headed back for San Molinas."

"If she goes there," Mason said, "she'll put her neck in a noose."

"Well, I think she's done it. She's probably there by this time."

"What did you do," Mason asked, "when you found she was gone?"

"I telephoned Paul Drake's office right away and told them to get in touch with you. I tried to locate you myself, but couldn't find you anywhere."

"I went uptown for breakfast, and then stopped in at a barber shop," Mason told her.

"Well," she said, "I think Paul Drake's on the job. I finally got him personally, and explained to him what had happened, and told him to have his men in San Molinas try and pick her up and keep her out of sight."

"What did Drake say?" Mason asked.

"Drake," she said with a wan smile, "didn't seem overly enthusiastic. I guess I caught him before he'd had his morning coffee. He seemed to think that he'd be dragged up before the Grand Jury in San Molinas if he tried anything like that."

"Did you sell *him* on the idea?" Mason asked.

"I sold him," she said grimly, "but I had to get pretty tough with him, in order to do it. He . . ." She broke off, as Drake's code knock sounded on the door, and said, "There he is now."

Mason nodded to her, and she crossed the office toward the door, then turned and said, "My eyes are a sight; let him in, will you, and let me go splash some cold water on my face?"

Mason nodded. As she glided through the door into the law library, Mason opened the corridor door. "Hi, Paul," he said.

Drake's shoulders were slumped forward, his manner lugubrious. "H'lo, Perry," he said, walking across to the big leather chair, and sliding into it sideways in his favorite position.

"What's new?" Mason asked.

"Plenty," Drake said.

"Good, bad, or indifferent?" Mason asked.

"It depends on what you consider indifferent," Drake said, mustering a slow grin. "To begin with, Perry, your certified copy of the divorce decree is an absolute forgery, and *that* was a damned clever stroke of genius, good enough for a cool one hundred thousand bucks."

"You're certain?" Mason asked.

"Absolutely certain. Mrs. Sabin probably had some Reno lawyer helping her, but we'll never find out who it was, of course, because it's a slick scheme of obtaining money under false pretenses. They had the regular printed blanks all in proper form, the signature of the clerk, and the deputy, and quite apparently they managed to get a genuine imprint of the court seal. That *could* have been done, the clerk admits, by sneaking around behind the counter sometime when he was occupied, but they don't let every Tom, Dick and Harry go behind the counter; so, evidently, it was pretty carefully worked out in advance."

"Then there wasn't any case of Sabin *vs.* Sabin ever filed?"

"No."

"That," Mason said, "was clever. If it hadn't been for this murder, no one would ever have detected that forgery. A certified copy of a decree of divorce is accepted at face value everywhere. Unless there's some question of the pleadings, no one ever thinks of going back to look at the court records. What a sweet job that was. A cool hundred thousand, and still his legal wife! Of course, there's the forgery angle and obtaining money under false pretenses; but if it hadn't been for this murder, no one would ever have tumbled to it."

"Even as it is, she's doing pretty well for herself," Drake said. "She's the legal widow, and, as such, entitled to step in and take charge."

"All right," Mason said, "we'll skip that for a while. What's this about Helen Monteith?"

Drake made a wry grimace and said, "I wish you'd wash your own dirty linen, Perry."

"Why?" Mason asked.

"It's bad enough to *hold* your coat while you cut the legal corners," Drake said, "but when I find myself suddenly wished into the position of *wearing* your coat, it doesn't go over so big."

Mason grinned, offered a desk humidor to the detective, and helped himself to a cigarette. "Go on," he said, lighting up, "give me the works."

"Della called the agency about quarter past eight this morning, and was in an awful lather," Drake said. "She wanted to get in touch with me, and wanted to get in touch with you, and wanted operatives to watch for Helen Monteith in San Molinas. My agency got in touch with me, and I telephoned Della at the number she'd left. She was registered under the name of Edith Fontayne. She told me all about Helen Monteith taking a run-out powder, and how you wanted her kept away from the police, and for me to beat it down to San Molinas and pick her up, and keep her hidden out.

"I told her to get in touch with you.

"She said she didn't know where you were. I told her I'd try and find you, and that was every damn thing I *would* do. My gosh, here I was remonstrating with you last night about the chances *you* were taking in holding a fugitive from justice away from the sheriff and the district attorney, and then all of a sudden Della proposes that I stick *my* neck out on the same proposition. It was so hot that even you had to play it so you didn't know where she was. . . ."

"What did you finally do?" Mason interrupted.

"Do?" Drake groaned. "What the devil *could* I do? I did exactly what she wanted. My God, Perry, I've always been friendly with Della, and it's been sort of a give-and-take, informal relationship. I always felt she was my friend, but when I told her I had to draw the line some place, she became a regular little hellcat over the wire. She told me that if I wanted your business, I was to take care of it the way you wanted; that I should know damn well you wouldn't leave me out on the end of a limb, and that you'd never made a foolish move yet; that you wanted Helen Monteith kept away from the police, and . . ."

"Never mind what she told you," Mason said, grinning, "what did you do?"

"Took my medicine like a little man, got my operatives in San Molinas on the telephone, and told them to get out to Helen Monteith's house; to grab her as soon as she showed up, and rush her back to the city; to kidnap her, if they had to, or do anything else that was necessary. My operatives started arguing with me, and I had to read the riot act to them, and told them I'd take the responsibility."

"Well," Mason said, "where's Helen Monteith now?"

"In jail," Drake said gloomily.

"How come?"

"My operatives didn't get the message in time. She'd got out to the house about half an hour before they did. Evidently, the police had left word with Mrs. Winters to let them know as soon as Helen Monteith showed up. The sheriff and the district attorney went out there on the run. They nabbed Helen. She'd been killing parrots, burning papers, and trying to find some place to hide a box of forty-one caliber cartridges. . . . You can figure where that puts *her*."

"How about the parrot-killing?" Mason asked with interest.

"She went home and killed the parrot," Drake said. "Snickasneed its head off with a butcher knife—made a nice clean job of it, too."

"As *soon* as she got home?" Mason asked.

"I reckon so. The sheriff didn't tumble to it for a little while. They caught her red-handed with the forty-one caliber shells and stuff she'd been burning in the fireplace. The sheriff went to quite a bit of trouble trying to get something out of the ashes, but about all he could tell was she'd been burning paper. They hustled her out to jail and telephoned in for a technical man from the homicide squad here, to see what could be done about reconstructing the papers. . . . Sergeant Holcomb has been working hand and glove with 'em, you know."

"I know," Mason said. "What did she say about the forty-one caliber shells? Does she admit buying them?"

"I don't know," Drake said. "They hustled her off to jail, and that's all anyone knows."

"When did they find out about the parrot?"

"Not so very long ago," Drake said. "Sergeant Holcomb's men apparently discovered *that* when they went through the house. . . ."

"Wait a minute," Mason interpolated. "Couldn't the parrot have been killed *after* Helen Monteith was arrested?"

"Not a chance," Drake said; "they put the place under guard right after they'd pinched her. That was so no one could get in and remove any evidence. I think your friend, Helen Watkins Sabin, may have been back of that move. I understand they're going through the house with a magnifying glass, looking for additional evidence. They found out about the parrot, and my man telephoned in a report about fifteen minutes ago. . . . Perry, why the devil do you suppose she killed that parrot?"

"The murder of a parrot," Mason said, with his eyes twinkling, "is somewhat similar to the murder of a human being; that is, a person must look for a motive. Having found a motive, there must then be opportunity, and . . ."

"Nix on it, nix on it," Drake interrupted. "Cut the comedy, Perry. *You* know damn well why she killed that parrot. Now, *I* want to know why."

"What makes you think I know?" Mason asked.

"Phooey!" Drake exclaimed, "don't take me for such a simp. She wanted the parrot out of the way, and you wanted the parrot preserved as evidence of something or other. You knew she was going to kill that parrot if she had a chance, so you had Della keep Helen Monteith out of the way long enough for us to go down and substitute parrots. I suppose it was because of the cracks the parrot's making about 'Drop that gun, Helen' and 'My God, you've shot me,' but I still don't see why she didn't kill the parrot before, instead of waiting until she had to climb down a fire escape to do the parrot-butchering. . . . I admit that I thought last night you were trying to keep Helen Monteith concealed from the authorities, and I thought so this morning when Della Street rang up. I didn't realize until just now that what you were really trying to do was to keep her away from that parrot."

"Well," Mason said, "now that the parrot's dead, we might as well . . ."

"But the parrot isn't dead," Drake interrupted. "You have the parrot. I suppose that the parrot is a witness to something or other—probably the murder—but damned if I see how he could have been. Tell me, Perry, could a parrot be used as a witness in a court of justice?"

"I don't know," Mason said. "It's an interesting point, Paul. I'm afraid the oath couldn't be administered to a parrot. In other words, he *might* commit perjury."

Drake glanced sidelong at Mason and said, "Go ahead and joke all you want to, brother. I suppose if you don't want to tell me, there's nothing I can do to make you."

"What else do you know?" Mason asked, abruptly changing the subject.

"Oh, a few things," Drake said. "I've had a bunch of men working all night. I've been trying to find out as much as I could about that wire-tapping up there at the cabin. You know, it occurred to me, Perry, that I might find out something about the calls which had been listened in on, by getting a copy of the telephone bill. You see, that cabin line is on a local exchange, but Sabin wouldn't have been interested in maintaining a telephone to call any of his neighbors. All of his contacts were in the city, and, of course, they'd have to be handled as long distance calls."

"A good idea," Mason said. "You deserve credit for that, Paul."

"Credit, hell," Drake said lugubriously. "I deserve cash for it. When you get the bill, it's going to floor you, Perry. I've got men working on overlapping nine-hour shifts, and I've got 'em scattered all over the country."

"That's fine," Mason said. "How did you get the telephone bill, Paul?"

"One of the men took a chance," Drake said, "went down to the telephone office, said he was a 'detective,' and, because of the murder, wanted service discontinued on the telephone, and wanted to pay the bill. The girl in the local telephone office fell for it, and handed him the bill. He insisted on checking all the long distance charges."

"What did you find?" Mason asked.

"A few calls to his residence, here in the city," Drake said. "Those were evidently calls where he'd talked with his secretary. Several of them had been station-to-station calls, and quite a few of them had been for Richard Waid personally. But the interesting things, Perry, are the person-to-person Reno calls."

"The Reno calls?" Mason asked.

"Yes. Apparently he was in almost daily telephone communication with his wife in Reno."

"What about?" Mason asked.

"You've got me on that," Drake said. "Probably trying to make certain that the divorce was going through according to schedule, and that she'd be in New York with a certified copy of the decree."

Della Street, her face freshly powdered, eyes showing but little trace of tears, bustled busily into the office, and appeared surprised to see Paul Drake. "Hi, Paul," she said.

"Don't you 'Hi, Paul' me, you baggage," Drake grumbled. "Of all the high-pressure stuff I ever had handed me ..."

She came over to where he was sitting on the chair, and put her hand on his arm. "Don't be such an old grouch-face," she laughed.

"Grouch-face nothing," he told her. "You put it up to me cold-turkey that I either had to go in for kidnapping or lose Mason's business."

"Well, Paul," she said, "I was trying to do what the Chief wanted—that is, what I thought he'd want under the circumstances."

Drake said to Mason, "You're bad enough. This girl is twice that bad."

Mason grinned at Della. "Don't talk with him this morning, Della, he's suffering from an ingrowing disposition."

"Did he get Helen Monteith?" she asked.

"No, the officers did," Mason told her.

"Oh!" she exclaimed in startled dismay.

"It's all right, Della," Mason said. "Ring up Sabin's residence, get Richard Waid or Charles Sabin, whichever one is available; say that I'd like to see both of them at the office at their earliest convenience."

He turned back to Paul Drake. "Have your men found out anything about where those forty-one caliber shells were bought, Paul?"

"Not *where* they were bought," Drake said, "but by this time the police sure have found out *who* bought 'em."

Mason dismissed it with a gesture. "Concentrate for a while on the Reno end of things, Paul. Find out as much as you can about what Mrs. Sabin did in Reno, and get me copies of the long distance telephone bill."

"Okay," Drake said, sliding from the chair, "and remember this, Perry Mason, the next time you duck out because things are getting too hot for *you* to handle, *I'm* going to duck out too. Being a stooge is all right, but being pushed up into the front-line trenches just when the machine guns start rattling, is a gray horse of another color."

CHAPTER NINE

IT WAS shortly after eleven when Charles W. Sabin and Richard Waid reached Mason's office. Mason wasted but little time in preliminaries. "I have some news," he said, "which may be of interest to you. As I told you last night, I had located Casanova. He was in the possession of a Helen Monteith, whom Fremont C. Sabin apparently married under the name of George Wallman. The parrot in her house was killed sometime either last night or early this morning. The theory of the police is that Helen Monteith killed him. The parrot had been saying re-

peatedly, 'Put down that gun, Helen . . . don't shoot. . . .
My God, you've shot me.'

"Now then," Mason went on, glancing from one to the
other, "does that mean anything to you?"

"It must mean the parrot was present at the time my
father was murdered," Sabin said. "Then Helen must
have . . . but which Helen?"

"But another parrot was found in the cabin," Mason
pointed out.

"Perhaps the murderer switched parrots," Waid ven-
tured.

Charles Sabin said, "Before we discuss that, I have
something of prime importance to take up with you."

"Go ahead," Mason told him, "we'll let the parrot
wait."

"I've found a will," Sabin announced.

"Where?"

"You remember it was disclosed that C. William Desmond acted as attorney for my father in connection with
certain matters pertaining to the divorce settlement. That
was news to me; I hadn't heard of it. It wasn't until Waid
told me that I knew anything about it.

"However, it seems that my father didn't care to have
Cutter, Grayson & Bright represent him in connection
with the divorce matter."

"And he had Desmond draw up a will at the same time
he made the property settlement agreement?" Mason
asked.

"Yes."

"What was the will?" Mason wanted to know.

Charles Sabin took a leather-backed notebook from his
pocket, and said, "I have made a copy of so much of the
provisions as relate to the distribution of his property. It
reads as follows:

" 'Because I have this day entered into an agreement
with my wife, Helen Watkins Sabin, by which it is agreed
and understood that she is to receive the sum of one
hundred thousand dollars in cash from me, by way of a
complete property settlement, and which said sum is to be
paid on the completion of divorce proceedings, and the

99

delivery of a certified copy of a final decree of divorce, I direct that, in the event I should die before said sum of one hundred thousand dollars is paid to my said wife, Helen Watkins Sabin, that then, and in such event, my said wife is to receive, from such estate as I may leave, the sum of one hundred thousand dollars in cash. In the event, however, said sum of cash has so been paid to the said Helen Watkins Sabin prior to the time of my death, I then intentionally make no other provision for her in this, my will, because the said sum of one hundred thousand dollars is ample to provide for her, and adequately compensate her for any claims she may have on my bounty, or to my estate.

" 'All of the rest, residue, and remainder of my estate, real, personal, or mixed, I give, devise, and bequeath, share and share alike, to my beloved son, Charles W. Sabin, who has, for years, maintained a commendable patience toward the vagaries of an eccentric man, who has ceased to regard the dollar as the ultimate goal of human endeavor, and to my beloved brother, Arthur George Sabin, who will probably not care to be made the object of my bounty.' "

Sabin glanced up from the notebook. "Suppose Dad died before the divorce was granted, does that," he asked, "have any effect on his will?"

"No," Mason said. "The way the will is drawn, Helen Watkins Sabin is completely washed up. Tell me about this brother."

"I don't know very much about Uncle Arthur," Charles Sabin said. "I have never seen him, but I understand, generally, he's something of an eccentric. I know that after Dad became wealthy, he offered Uncle Arthur an opportunity to come into the business, and Uncle Arthur indignantly refused it. After that, Dad visited him and became very much impressed with Uncle Arthur's philosophy of life. I think that something of my father's detachment from active business was due to the influence of Uncle Arthur, and I think that's what he means in his will. . . . Of course, you understand, Mr. Mason, that I want to make some independent provision for my father's widow?"

"You mean Helen Watkins Sabin?" Mason asked in surprise.

"No, I mean Helen Monteith, or Helen Wallman, or whatever her legal name is. Somehow, I regard her as being my father's widow, and much more entitled to recognition, as such, than the fortune hunter who hypnotized Dad into matrimony. Incidentally, Mr. Mason, Wallman is a family name. My own middle name is Wallman. That's probably why my father used it."

"Well," Mason said, "as it happens, Helen Monteith, as we may as well call her, is in custody in San Molinas. The authorities intend to charge her with the murder of your father."

Sabin said, "That's one of the things I want to talk with you about, Mr. Mason. I want to ask you, fairly and frankly, if *you* think she murdered my father."

Mason said, "I'm virtually certain that she didn't murder him, but there's some circumstantial evidence which she's going to have a hard time explaining away—in fact, she may never be able to do it, unless we uncover the real murderer."

"What evidence, for instance?" Sabin asked.

"In the first place," Mason said, "she has motivation. She'd been tricked into a bigamous marriage. Men have been killed for less than that. She had opportunity; and what's more, she had the weapon.

"That's the worst of circumstantial evidence. The prosecuting attorney has at his command all the facilities of organized investigation. He uncovers facts. He selects only those which, in his opinion, are significant. Once he's come to the conclusion the defendant is guilty, the only facts he considers significant are those which point to the guilt of the defendant. That's why circumstantial evidence is such a liar. Facts themselves are meaningless. It's only the interpretation we give those facts which counts."

"We've had some significant facts develop out at the house," Waid said, glancing across at Charles Sabin. "Did you intend to tell Mr. Mason about Mrs. Sabin and Steve?"

Sabin said, "Thank you, Richard, for calling it to my attention. After you left last night, Mr. Mason, Steve Watkins and his mother were in the mother's room in deep consultation. They left the house about midnight and haven't returned since. They didn't leave any word where they were going, and we haven't been able to locate them. The coroner at San Molinas had called an inquest for eight o'clock this evening, and the funeral is scheduled for tomorrow at two o'clock. Having Mrs. Sabin missing is, of course, embarrassing to the family. I consider her departure evidence of shocking bad taste."

Mason looked across at Waid. "Did you tell Sheriff Barnes and Sergeant Holcomb anything about this business you were transacting for Mr. Sabin in New York?"

"No, I only told them what I considered entered into the case. On this other matter, I didn't tell a soul until last night. Mrs. Sabin had browbeaten me into silence."

"You told the sheriff about receiving a telephone call from Mr. Sabin at ten o'clock at night?"

"Yes, of course. I felt that entered into the case and wasn't betraying any confidence."

"Did Mr. Sabin seem in good spirits when you talked with him?"

"In excellent spirits. I don't think I've ever heard his voice sound happier. Looking back on it now, of course, I can understand. He'd just received word that Mrs. Sabin was going to get the divorce decree the next day, and that gave him the chance to remarry Miss Monteith. Mrs. Sabin had evidently telephoned him and told him that the divorce was going through."

"Did you know that he was spending some time in San Molinas?" Mason asked.

"Yes, I did," Waid admitted. "I knew he was there quite a bit of the time. He telephoned to me several times from San Molinas."

"I knew that also," Charles Sabin interposed. "I didn't know what he was doing there, but Dad was peculiar that way. You know, he'd go into a community, completely lose his identity, take an assumed name, and just mingle with people."

"Have you any idea why he did it?" Mason asked. "That is, was he after anything in particular?"

"As to that, I couldn't say," Charles Sabin said. "Of course, in considering father's character, you must take into consideration certain things. He'd been a highly successful business man, as we judge standards of success; that is, he had amassed a comfortable fortune. He had nothing to gain by adding to his material wealth. I think he was, therefore, thoroughly ripe for some new suggestion. It happened to come through Uncle Arthur. Uncle Arthur lived somewhere in Kansas—at least he did two or three years ago, when father visited him; and I know that his philosophies made a profound impression on Dad. After Dad returned, he said that we were all too greedy; that we worshiped the dollar as the goal of our success; that it was a false goal; that man should concentrate more on trying to develop his character.

"You might be interested in his economic philosophy, Mr. Mason. He believed men attached too much importance to money as such. He believed a dollar represented a token of work performed, that men were given these tokens to hold until they needed the product of work performed by some other man, that anyone who tried to get a token without giving his best work in return was an economic counterfeiter. He felt that most of our depression troubles had been caused by a universal desire to get as many tokens as possible in return for as little work as possible—that too many men were trying to get lots of tokens without doing *any* work. He said men should cease to think in terms of tokens and think, instead, only in terms of work performed as conscientiously as possible."

"Just how did he figure the depression was caused, in terms of tokens?" Mason asked, interested.

"By greed," Sabin said. "Everyone was gambling, trying to get tokens without work. Then afterward, when tokens ceased to represent honest work, men hated to part with them. A man who had performed slipshod work in return for a token hated to part with that token in exchange for the products of slipshod labor on the part of another laborer. In other words, the token itself came to mean more than what it could be exchanged for—or people thought it did, because too many people had become economic counterfeiters."

"That's interesting," Mason said. "By the way, how many people lived in the house?"

"Only two of us, Mr. Waid and I."

"Servants?"

"One housekeeper is all. After Mrs. Sabin left for her world tour, we closed up virtually all the house, and let the servants go. I didn't realize why that was done at the time, but, of course, I understand now that Dad knew Helen Watkins Sabin wouldn't return, and was intending to close up the house."

"And the parrot?" Mason asked. "Did your father take the parrot with him on his trips?"

"Most of the time the parrot was with Dad. There were times when he left it home—with Mrs. Sabin, mostly. Incidentally, Mrs. Sabin was very much attached to the parrot."

Mason turned to Waid. "Did Steve have any motive for murder, any hatred of Mr. Sabin?"

"Steve himself *couldn't* have murdered Mr. Sabin," Waid said positively. "I know that Mr. Sabin was alive at ten o'clock Monday night, the fifth of September. Steve and I left for New York right after I'd received that telephone call. We didn't arrive in New York until late Tuesday afternoon. You see, there's a four-hour time difference, what with the difference in sun time and the additional hour of daylight saving time."

Mason said, "The certified decree of divorce, which Mrs. Sabin handed you in New York, was a forgery."

"Was *what?*" Waid exclaimed, startled.

"A forgery," Mason repeated.

"Look here, Mr. Mason, that decree was passed on by Mr. Sabin's New York attorneys."

"It was perfectly legal *in form*," Mason admitted. "In fact, it was all worked out to the last detail, even the name of the clerk and the deputy. A very clever forgery—but nevertheless the document was forged."

"How did you find that out?" Sabin asked, highly excited.

Mason said, "I made it my business to investigate the court records. I gave a photostatic copy of the decree to a detective who flew to Reno. The case was purportedly a default matter, and handled in a routine manner. Much to my surprise, when I investigated, I found that there were no court records of any divorce."

"Good heavens," Charles Sabin said, "what did she expect to gain by that? She must have known she'd be discovered."

"On the other hand," Mason said, "under ordinary circumstances, no one would ever look back at a certified copy of a divorce decree. It would have been rather a safe forgery."

"But why did she want to rely on a forged document?" Sabin asked.

"I don't know," Mason told him. "There are several guesses. One of them is that there's some question as to the validity of her marriage to your father."

"But why should that have kept her from filing suit for divorce?" Waid asked.

"Because," Mason said, "regardless of the optimistic ideas of Fremont C. Sabin, there was bound to have been publicity. Newspapers keep highly trained investigators stationed at Reno for the purpose of scrutinizing divorce actions. They're particularly anxious to find out if any of the movie celebrities slip over to Reno for the purpose of getting a divorce under their true names, and without disclosing their Hollywood identities. Now if, perhaps, Helen Watkins Sabin had another husband living, from whom she'd never been divorced . . . well, she wouldn't have dared to risk the publicity. There was a hundred thousand dollars at stake—and that's a considerable stake."

Sabin said, "If there's anything illegal about that first marriage, then how about the marriage ceremony my father went through with Helen Monteith in Mexico?"

"Now," Mason said, with a grin, "you're getting into the *real* legal problem."

"What's the answer?" Sabin asked.

"That," Mason told him, "depends very much on what we can find out by examining Helen Watkins Sabin on the witness stand. Suppose, Mr. Sabin, you attend the inquest at San Molinas tonight. I think the sheriff will be broad-minded enough to see that a complete investigation is made. Some interesting facts should be uncovered."

The telephone on Mason's unlisted private wire buzzed sharply. Mason picked up the receiver to hear Paul Drake's voice saying, "Are you busy right now, Perry?"

"Yes."

"Anyone there in connection with this case?"

"Yes."

"I think," Drake said, "you'd better arrange to meet me outside the office."

"That won't be necessary," Mason said. "The clients who are in the office are just finishing up their business. I'll see you in just a moment or two."

He hung up the telephone and extended his hand to Sabin. "I'm glad to learn about that will," he said.

"And you'll let us know if anything new . . . well, if you . . . I mean if you hear anything about Helen Watkins Sabin, let me know what she's doing, will you?"

"She's probably keeping under cover," Mason told him, "until she can find out what's going to be done about that forged decree of divorce."

"Not that woman," Charles Sabin said. "You'll never get *her* on the defensive. She's busy somewhere right now, stirring up a whole mess of trouble for us."

Mason ushered them out through the exit door. "Well," he said, with a smile, "at least she's energetic."

As his visitors turned the corner in the corridor, Mason stood in the door, waiting for Drake. The detective appeared within a matter of seconds. "Coast clear?" he asked.

"The coast is clear," Mason told him, ushering him into the room. "I've just had a session with Charles Sabin and Richard Waid, the secretary. What do you know, Paul?"

"You wanted the long distance telephone calls which had been put in from the cabin," Drake said. "Well, I've had men breaking down numbers into names. Here's what we find. The last call of which there's any record came through on the afternoon of Monday the fifth at

106

about four o'clock. Now as I understand it, the secretary says that when Sabin called him at ten o'clock, he reported the telephone at the cabin was out of order. Is that right?"

Mason nodded.

"Well," Drake said, "if the telephone was out of order, Sabin couldn't put in any calls and couldn't send out any calls. Do you get what I mean?"

"No, I don't," Mason told him. "Go on and spill it."

"Well," Drake said. "Something happened to cause Sabin to send Waid to New York. We don't know what that something was. We don't know where the pay station was that Sabin telephoned from, but in all probability it was the nearest one to the cabin. We can tell more when we check up on calls; but suppose that it was twenty minutes or half an hour away from the cabin."

"What are you getting at?" Mason asked.

"Simply this," Drake said. "If the telephone was out of order from four o'clock on, and Sabin telephoned Waid to go to New York, Sabin must have received some information between the hours of four o'clock in the afternoon and probably nine-thirty at night which convinced him that Mrs. Sabin would be in New York on the evening of Wednesday the seventh to surrender a certified copy of the divorce decree and pick up the money.

"Now then how did he get that information? If the telephone was out of order, he couldn't have received it over the telephone. He evidently didn't have it at four o'clock. In other words, Perry, that information *must* have been obtained from someone who came to the cabin."

"Or sent Sabin a message," Mason said. "That's a good point, Paul. Of course, we don't *know* that the telephone went out of commission immediately after four o'clock."

"No," Drake said. "We don't, but on the other hand it's hardly probable that the telephone would have been in commission when Sabin received word that the divorce was going through all right and then gone out of commission as soon as he tried to telephone the news to Waid—which would have been immediately afterwards."

"You forget," Mason pointed out, his eyes narrowing

into thoughtful slits, "that the telephone line was tapped."

"By George, I do at that!" Drake exclaimed.

"Anything may happen on a tapped line," Mason said. "The wire-tappers could have thrown the telephone out of commission at a moment's notice, and may have done so."

"What would have been their object?" Drake asked.

"That," Mason said, "remains to be discovered."

"Well," Drake told him, "I thought you might be particularly interested in that four o'clock call because of what had happened."

"I am," Mason said. "Whom was it to?"

"To Randolph Bolding, the examiner of questioned documents."

Mason frowned. "Why the devil did Sabin want to ring up a handwriting expert?" he asked.

"You don't suppose he'd had a look at that certified decree of divorce and figured it was a forgery?" Drake asked.

"No," Mason said. "The decree wasn't dated until the sixth. If he'd seen it on the fifth, he'd have known it was a forgery."

"That's right," Drake admitted.

"Have you talked with Bolding?" Mason asked.

"One of my operatives did," Drake said, grinning, "and Bolding threw him out on his ear. Said that anything which had transpired between him and Sabin was a professional confidence. So I thought perhaps you'd better go down there, Perry, and talk him into being a good dog."

Mason reached for his hat. "On my way," he said.

CHAPTER TEN

RANDOLPH BOLDING had carefully cultivated an expression of what Mason had once described to a jury as "synthetic, professional gravity." His every move was calculated to impress any audience he might have with the fact that he was one of the leading exponents of an exact science.

He bowed from the hips. "How do you do, Mr. Mason," he said.

Mason walked on into the private office and sat down. Bolding carefully closed the door, seated himself behind the huge desk, smoothed down his vest, mechanically adjusted papers on the blotter, giving his visitor an opportunity to look at the enlarged photomicros of questioned signatures which adorned the walls.

Mason said abruptly, "You were doing some work for Fremont C. Sabin, Bolding?"

Bolding raised his eyes. They were bulging, moist eyes which held no expression. "I prefer not to answer that question."

"Why?"

"My relations with my clients are professional secrets— just as yours are."

Mason said, "I'm representing Charles Sabin."

"That means nothing to me," Bolding said.

"As Fremont C. Sabin's heir, Charles Sabin is entitled to any information you have."

"I think not."

"To whom *will* you communicate this information?"

"To no one."

Mason crossed his long legs and settled back in the chair. "Charles Sabin," he said, "wanted me to tell you that he thought your bill was too high."

The handwriting expert blinked his moist eyes several times in rapid succession. "But I haven't submitted one yet," he said.

"I know; but Sabin thinks it's too high."

"Well, what's that got to do with it?"

"Sabin," Mason said, "will probably be the executor of the estate."

"But how can he say my bill is too high when he doesn't know how much it is?"

Mason shrugged his shoulders. "That," he said, "is something you'll have to take up with Sabin. Of course, you know how it is, Bolding. If an executor approves the charge against the estate, it goes right through. If he doesn't approve it, then you have to bring suit to establish your claim. In case you don't know it, it's a long way to Tipperary."

Bolding gazed down at the blotter on his desk for several thoughtful seconds.

Mason stretched, yawned prodigiously, and said, "Well, I guess I'll be going. I've got lots of work to do."

"Wait a minute," Bolding said, as Mason rose to start toward the door. "That attitude isn't fair."

"Probably not," Mason agreed carelessly. "However, Sabin is my client and that's what he says. You understand how it is dealing with clients, Bolding. We have to follow our client's wishes and instructions."

"But it's so manifestly unfair," Bolding protested.

"I don't think it is," Mason said.

"You don't?"

"No."

"Why not?"

"Because," Mason told him, "you aren't submitting a bill to Fremont C. Sabin for anything you did for him personally, you're submitting a bill to the estate for things which were done to conserve the property during Sabin's lifetime . . . at least, I suppose that's the theory of it."

"That's the theory of it," Bolding agreed.

"Well," Mason said, "you haven't conserved anything."

Bolding flushed. "I can't help it if a man dies before he carries out his plans."

"No," Mason observed, "I daresay you can't. However, that would seem to be your loss, not ours. You've lost a client."

"But under the law, I'm entitled to recover compensation for my services. A thousand dollars is a most reasonable charge."

"Go right ahead," Mason told him, "and recover your compensation. I was simply giving you a friendly tip that Sabin thinks your charges are too high. He'll probably bring in a couple of the other experts, who have been waiting to take a rap at you, and have them testify that your fees are outrageous."

"Are you trying to blackmail me?" Bolding asked.

"Just warning you," Mason said.

"What do you want?"

"Me?" Mason asked, surprised. "Why *I* don't want anything."

"What does Sabin want?"

"I don't know," Mason told him. "You'll be getting in touch with Sabin when you present your bill. You can ask him then."

"I'll ask him nothing."

"Okay by me," Mason said. "Sabin thinks your charges are plain robbery. He says that whatever you did, you did for Mr. Sabin and not for the estate."

"I am doing it for the estate."

"I don't see how," Mason said.

"You'd have to understand what it was all about in order to see that," Bolding said.

"Doubtless," Mason admitted, "if I knew all the facts, I'd feel differently about it. Doubtless, if Sabin knew all the facts, he'd feel differently about it. You see, he doesn't know all the facts, and there's no likelihood he'll learn them—in time to do the estate any good."

"You're putting me in a very difficult position, Mason," Bolding said irritably.

Mason's voice showed surprise. "I am? Why, I thought you'd put yourself in it."

Bolding pushed back his swivel chair, crossed over to a steel filing case, unlocked the catch and angrily jerked the steel drawer open. "Oh, all right," he said, "if you're going to act that way about it."

Bolding opened the files and spread papers out on the desk. "Richard Waid," he said, "was Fremont C. Sabin's secretary. He held Sabin's power of attorney and had authority to sign checks up to five thousand dollars. Checks over five thousand dollars had to be signed by Sabin. I have in this file sixteen thousand five hundred dollars in forged checks. The checks are three in number, each is over five thousand in amount, and each purports to have been signed by Sabin. The forgeries were so clever the bank cashed them."

"How were they discovered?" Mason asked.

"Sabin discovered them when he audited his bank account."

"Why didn't Waid discover them?"

"Because Sabin had the habit of issuing checks from time to time without advising his secretary."

"Did Waid finally learn of these checks?"

"No, Mr. Sabin wanted it kept a closely guarded secret, because he thought it was a family matter."

"Just what," Mason asked, "do you mean by that?"

Bolding said, "Perhaps I can quote from Mr. Sabin's letter to me, and it will explain matters more clearly." He picked up a typewritten letter, turned over the first page and read from the second page:

" 'I suppose it will be difficult for you to detect any handwriting characteristics of the forger from the signature itself. However, it occurs to me that the payees are probably fictitious, that the endorsements on the back of the check will give you something on which to work. I am, therefore, enclosing herewith, in addition to the checks, a letter written to me by Steven Watkins. Inasmuch as this young man is the son of my wife, you can appreciate the importance of regarding the entire matter as most confidential. Under no circumstances must there be any newspaper publicity. The bank is sworn to secrecy. I am saying nothing at this end. Therefore, if there should be any disclosure, I will know that it was brought about through an indiscretion on your part.

" 'As soon as you have arrived at an opinion, please advise me by telephone. I will be in my mountain cabin at least by Monday, the fifth, and will remain there for several days.' "

"What conclusions did you reach?" Mason asked.

"The checks are clever forgeries. They are free-hand forgeries; that is, the signatures were dashed off at high speed by a competent and daring forger. There are no tremors in the signatures. The signatures were not traced. There is no evidence of the painfully laborious handwriting of the slow, clumsy forger who must rely upon tracing. Such signatures look quite all right to the naked eye, but under the microscope look quite different from the smooth, fast-flowing lines of a quickly executed signature such as these."

"I understand," Mason said.

"The forged signature *may* be the work of Steven Watkins, the young man whose handwriting was sent me by Mr. Sabin. I don't know. I am inclined to think the endorsements, however, were not made by young Watkins. In fact, they have all the earmarks of being genuine signatures, although they *may* have been fictitious."

"How were the checks cashed?"

"They were put through various banks for collection, in each instance by a person who opened an account, let it remain for a week or two, and then drew out the entire balance. The references, addresses, etc., in each instance were fabricated."

"And you don't think Watkins did it?"

"To be frank," Bolding said, "I do not . . . That is, the endorsements on the checks. As to the forgery of the signature, I cannot say."

"Did you so advise Mr. Sabin?"

"Yes."

"When?"

"On Friday, the second of September. He was in the city and called on me for a brief conference."

"Then what?" Mason asked.

"He said he would think it over and let me know."

"Did he?"

"Yes."

"When?"

"About four o'clock on Monday, September fifth. It was a holiday, but I happened to be in my office. Sabin caught me here on a long distance telephone call."

"Did he say where he was?"

"He said he was in his mountain cabin."

"What did he say?"

"He said, he'd been thinking over the matter of those forgeries and said he was sending me other handwriting specimens in a letter which he would mail that afternoon."

"Did you ever receive the letter?" Mason asked.

"No."

"Then you gather that he didn't mail it?"

"I think that's a reasonable inference."

"Do you know why he didn't mail it?"

"No. He may have changed his mind; he may have postponed it, or he may have entered into some transaction . . . perhaps some property settlement . . . which was conditioned upon the fact . . . Well, you may draw your own conclusions."

"What gives you that idea?" Mason asked.

"Certain circumstances which I am not at liberty to divulge."

Mason said, "Under the circumstances, Bolding, it would seem that your services have been of the greatest value to the estate. I would advise the executor to honor your bill."

Bolding said, without enthusiasm, "Thank you."

Mason said, "If you're in need of money, I might advance the money myself from my personal account and take payment of your claim in the regular course of administration."

Bolding said, "That would be most acceptable."

"Your bill was a thousand dollars?" Mason asked.

"Fifteen hundred," Bolding said.

"I would, of course, want to take possession of the documents in the case on behalf of the administrator," Mason said.

"That's understood."

Mason pulled out his checkbook, wrote a check for fifteen hundred dollars, scribbled an assignment of Bolding's bill on the back of the check, and passed it across to Bolding. "Your endorsement on the back of the check," he said, "will at once constitute a receipt for the amount of the money and an assignment of your claim against the estate."

"Thank you," Bolding said. He pocketed the check, took an envelope from the desk drawer, placed the checks and letters in it, and handed the envelope across to the lawyer. Then he arose, went to the door of the private office and held it open.

Mason heard the rapid, nervous *click . . . click . . .*

click of the high heels on a woman's shoes. He stepped back so that he was concealed behind the jamb of the door as he heard Helen Watkins Sabin say, "I bet you didn't think I was going to come back with the cash, did you, Mr. Bolding? Well, here it is, one thousand dollars, ten one-hundred-dollar bills. Now, if you'll give me a receipt, I'll take the documents and . . ."

Bolding said, "You'll pardon me, Mrs. Sabin, but would you mind going around to the other office. I have a client here."

"Oh, well," she said, "your client can go right on out. He doesn't need to mind me. You were standing there in the door to usher him out, so you can just usher me in."

She swept past Bolding into the office, and then suddenly whirled to face Perry Mason.

"You!" she said.

Mason bowed.

"What are you doing here?" she asked.

"Collecting evidence," Mason told her.

"Evidence of what?"

"Evidence of what may have been a motive for the murder of Fremont C. Sabin."

"Bosh," she said. "Mr. Bolding doesn't have any such evidence."

"You are familiar with what he has then?" Mason asked.

"I didn't come here to be cross-examined," she said. "I have some business to transact with Mr. Bolding, and I don't care to have you present at my conversation."

"Very well," Mason said, and bowed himself out into the corridor.

He had just reached the elevator when he heard a door open and close with a violent bang. He heard running feet in the corridor and turned to find Mrs. Sabin bearing down upon him with ominous purpose.

"You got those papers from Bolding," she charged.

"Indeed," Mason said.

"You boosted the ante five hundred dollars and took those documents. Well, you can't get away with it. You have no right to them. I'm Fremont's widow. I'm entitled to everything in the estate. Give me those papers at once."

"There is some doubt," Mason told her, "about just who will be settling up the estate. There is even some doubt about your being Fremont Sabin's widow."

"You tangle with me," she said, "and you'll be sorry. I want those papers, and I'm going to get them. You can save time by turning them over to me now."

"But I see no reason to save time," Mason told her, smiling coldly. "*I'm* not in a hurry."

Her eyes glittered with the intensity of her feeling. "You," she said, "are going to try to frame something on Steve. You can't make it stick. I'm warning you."

"Frame what on him?" Mason asked.

"You know perfectly well. Those forgeries."

Mason said, "I'm not framing anything on anybody. I'm simply taking charge of evidence."

"Well, you have no right to take charge of it. I'll take charge of it myself."

"Oh, no," Mason said, "I couldn't think of letting you do that. You might lose the forged checks. After all, this is rather a trying and exciting time, Mrs. Sabin. *If* you should mislay these checks and couldn't find them again, it would give the forger altogether too much of a break— particularly when we consider that the forger is, in all probability, the murderer."

"Bosh!" she said. "Helen Monteith murdered him! I found out all about her. However, I suppose you're quite capable of dragging Steve into it in order to save her, aren't you?"

Mason smiled and said, "Quite."

"Are you going to give me those checks?"

"No."

"You'll wish you had."

"By the way," Mason observed amiably, "the inquest is to be held tonight in San Molinas. I believe the sheriff has a subpoena for you, and . . ."

She stamped her foot. "It's just the same as larceny. I think there's a law covering that. All property belonging to the decedent . . ."

"Is a forged check property?" Mason asked.

"Well, I want them anyway."

"I gathered you did," Mason observed affably.

"Oh!" she exclaimed. "You . . . you . . . you . . ."

She launched herself at him, clawing at the envelope in the inside pocket of his coat. Mason pushed her easily aside and said, "That isn't going to get you anywhere, Mrs. Sabin."

A red light flashed as an elevator cage slid to a stop. Mason entered. "Coming, ma'am?" the elevator man asked Mrs. Sabin.

"No," she said, and turned on her heel to stride belligerently back toward the office of Randolph Bolding.

Mason rode down in the elevator and drove at once to a branch post office. He carefully sealed the envelope containing the forged checks and the various letters and addressed the envelope to Sheriff Barnes at San Molinas. He then placed postage stamps on the letter and dropped it in the mailchute.

CHAPTER ELEVEN

PERRY MASON, Della Street and Paul Drake rode three abreast in the front seat of Mason's car. The parrot was in the rear of the car, the cage partially covered with a lap robe.

Drake, looking at his wrist watch, said, "You're going to get there plenty early, Perry."

Mason said, "I want to talk with the sheriff and with Helen Monteith."

As Mason guided the car clear of the city traffic and hit the open highway, Drake said, "Well, it looks as though you had the right hunch on this divorce business, Perry. There's a pretty good chance Helen Watkins never was divorced from Rufus Watkins. We've found a witness who says Helen Watkins told her that she hadn't been divorced. That was two weeks before she started working for Fremont C. Sabin."

"Don't you suppose she got a divorce afterwards?" Mason inquired.

"I don't know, Perry, but I'm inclined to think she

didn't. You see, she was a resident of California. She couldn't leave in order to establish a residence elsewhere. If she'd secured a California divorce, she'd have had to wait a year for the interlocutory decree to become final, before she could have married again. That didn't suit her purpose at all. She had her hooks out for Sabin before she'd been working there three weeks."

"How about Rufus Watkins?" Mason asked. "Don't you suppose she could have arranged with him to get a divorce?"

"That," Drake said, "is the rub. She *may* have done so, but it looks as though she didn't do anything until after she'd married Sabin, and by that time Rufus was in a position to do a little fancy blackmail."

"Is that surmise?" Mason asked. "Or do you have some evidence to support it?"

"I can't tell just yet," Drake told him, "but it looks very much as though we had some evidence to support it. We got a tip that Helen Watkins Sabin's bank account showed quite a few checks payable to a Rufus W. Smith. We're trying to verify that, and find out about this Rufus W. Smith. We know that he answers the general description of Rufus Watkins, but we haven't as yet definitely established that they are one and the same."

Mason said, "That's good work, Paul. That gives us something to go on."

"Of course, Perry, there's quite a bit of stuff shaping up against Helen Monteith," Drake pointed out. "I understand, now, they've found a witness who saw her in the vicinity of the cabin about noon on the sixth."

"That," Mason admitted, "would be bad."

"Well, it may be just rumor," Drake said. "My operative in San Molinas picked it up."

Mason said, "We're going to go and see the sheriff as soon as we get there. He may be willing to put the cards on the table."

Della Street said, "Chief, she simply *can't* be guilty of murder. She *really* loved him."

"I know," Mason said, "but she certainly left a lot of circumstantial evidence hanging around loose . . . Incidentally, there's a nice legal point involved. If she actually *is* the widow of Fremont C. Sabin, then she inherits a share of his property, because the will is invalid as to her."

"How so?" Drake asked.

"A will," Mason said, "is revoked by the subsequent marriage of the testator. On the other hand, a will in which he makes no provision for his wife, and in which it appears that the omission was not intentional, is also subject to attack. The farther we go into this thing, Paul, the more possibilities it has."

They drove for several miles in thoughtful silence, then suddenly, from the back seat, came the hoarse voice of the parrot: "Put down that gun, Helen! Don't shoot! *Squawk. Squawk.* My God, you've shot me!"

Drake said, "We have two suspects in this case, both of them named Helen. Perry, if you introduce that parrot in evidence to show that Helen Watkins Sabin fired the shot, the district attorney will turn your own evidence against you to show that Helen Monteith did it."

Mason grinned, "That parrot may make a better witness than you think, Paul."

Sheriff Barnes had an office in the south wing of the old courthouse. Afternoon sunlight, beating through the windows, illuminated battered furniture, a floor covered with linoleum, which, in several spots, had been completely worn through. Bulletin boards on the wall were adorned with printed circulars of persons wanted for crime. Across from these posters, and on the wall on the opposite side of the room, were glass-framed display cases, in which various lethal weapons, which had figured in historic murder cases in the county, were on display.

Sheriff Barnes sat behind the old-fashioned roll-topped desk, in a dilapidated swivel chair, which squeaked monotonously as he teetered back and forth.

While Perry Mason talked, the sheriff slipped a plug of tobacco from his pants pocket, opened a knife, the blade of which had been rubbed thin through many sharpenings, and cut off a corner of moist, black tobacco.

When Mason had finished, the sheriff was silent for a few moments, rolling the tobacco over the edge of his tongue; then he shifted his steady, thoughtful eyes to the lawyer and said, "Those are all the facts you have?"

"That's a general summary of everything," Mason told him. "My cards are on the table."

"You shouldn't have done that about the telephone bill," the sheriff said to Paul Drake. "We had some trouble getting a duplicate telephone bill. It delayed things for us a little while."

"I'm sorry," Mason told him, "it was my fault. I'm assuming the responsibility."

The sheriff swung his weight slowly back and forth in the creaking chair. "What conclusions are you drawing?" he asked of Mason.

Mason said, "I don't think I'm ready to draw any conclusions yet. I'd like to wait until after the inquest."

"Think you could draw some then?"

"I think I could," Mason told him, "if I were permitted to question the witnesses."

"That's sort of up to the coroner, ain't it?" the sheriff asked.

"Yes," Mason said, "but it occurs to me the coroner might do what you suggested would be in the best interests of justice."

"I suppose he'd have to ask the district attorney about what he should do," the sheriff remarked musingly.

"In that event," Mason said, "we're sunk. That's why I said I didn't want to form any opinion from the evidence. Once a man forms an opinion, he starts interpreting facts in the light of that belief. He ceases to be an impartial judge of facts. That's what's happened to Raymond Sprague. He's come to the conclusion that I'm opposed to justice; that my tactics must necessarily be opposed to justice; that, therefore, he can best serve the ends of justice by blocking me at every turn. He's also come to the conclusion that Helen Monteith is guilty of murder; therefore, he interprets all the facts in the light of that belief."

"Ain't that being a little harsh on Sprague?" the sheriff asked.

"I don't think so," Mason replied. "After all he's only human."

The sheriff munched on his tobacco, then slowly nodded and said, "One of the things I've got against this state is the way they measure the efficiency of a district attorney. The state keeps records of the criminal trials in the different counties. They gauge the efficiency of the district attorneys by the percentage of convictions they secure in cases tried. Now that ain't right. If I was keeping a district attorney's record, I'd give him more points for finding out somebody was innocent, and not prosecuting that person, than I would for getting a conviction just because he'd gone into court."

Paul Drake started to say something, but Mason warned him to silence with a gesture.

"Of course," Sheriff Barnes went on, "Raymond Sprague has his record to consider. Sprague is a good boy, he wants to get some advancement politically. He knows that when he comes up for office, no matter what he runs for, people are going to look at his record as district attorney.

"Now, I'm different. I'm sheriff, and that's all I want to be—just sheriff. I know that I have a lot of power to use, and I want to use it fair and square to everyone. I don't want to have anyone convicted that ain't guilty."

"Under those circumstances," Mason said, "don't you think it would be more fair, all around, to have the guilt or innocence determined at the coroner's inquest tonight? Then, perhaps, it wouldn't be necessary to take the matter before a jury. If Helen Monteith *isn't* innocent, the prosecution has everything to gain by having me put all my facts before the coroner's jury. If she *is* innocent, then the prosecution has everything to gain by not being put in the position of going into court on a big case, and having the jury return a verdict of not guilty."

"Of course," the sheriff said, "if we was going to do that down at the coroner's inquest, we couldn't have a lot of objections and things; we'd have to scoot right along and hit the high spots. You couldn't make a lot of objections to questions and all that sort of stuff."

"I wouldn't," Mason promised.

"Well," the sheriff said, "I'll see what I can do."

"I'd prefer," Mason told him, "that you didn't try to do

121

anything with Sprague. In other words, I don't want to tip my hand to Sprague. I'm putting my cards on the table with you."

"Nope," the sheriff said, "I'm co-operating with the district attorney; the district attorney has to know everything about it. Maybe he'll be willing to give you a break. Maybe he won't. I'm telling you, fair and square, if he agrees to let you talk it'll be because he'll want to give you lots of rope and watch you hang yourself."

"That suits me," Mason said. "All I want is the rope."

"You'd have to be kinda tactful," the sheriff said. "Sprague wouldn't like it if it appeared you was bringing out all the evidence."

"I can appreciate that," Mason said. "I'd try to let it appear I was co-operating with the district attorney; whether I can really co-operate or not, depends upon how Sprague looks at it."

Sheriff Barnes looked out the window. The afternoon sunlight etched the lines of his bronzed countenance, showed the silver strands in his hair. He held his lips pursed for ten thoughtful seconds before seeking the relief of a cuspidor.

"Well," he said, "we'll see what we can do. As I understand it, all you want is to see that all the evidence gets before that coroner's jury."

"That's all," Mason said, "and I'd like to do it in such a way the coroner's jury would feel I was trying to assist the coroner. As I've mentioned before, when people get fixed beliefs, they interpret everything in the light of those beliefs. Take politics, for instance. We can look back at past events, and the deadly significance of those events seems so plain that we don't see how people could possibly have overlooked them. Yet millions of voters, at the time, saw those facts and warped their significance so that they supported erroneous political beliefs.

"The same is true of the things which are happening at present. A few years from now we'll look back in wonder that people failed to see the deadly significance of signs on the political horizon. Twenty years from now even the most stupid high school student can appreciate the importance of those signs and the results which must inevitably have followed. But right now we have some twenty-five million who think another. And both sides believe they're correctly interpreting the facts."

The sheriff came to an upright position, while the chair gave forth one long, last, protesting squeak, which made Della Street wince. "Well," he said, "I'll let you know in an hour or so. I'll have to talk with the coroner and the district attorney. Personally, Mason, I'm for you. I ain't running the prosecution, but I am running the department of criminal investigation. There's been a murder committed in my county. I'm going to do everything I can to find out who committed that murder. I think you're prejudiced because you think Helen Monteith is innocent, whereas I think she's guilty. Naturally, you're trying to protect your client. On the other hand, you've had a lot more experience with big murder cases than I have. I ain't going to let you lead me around by the nose, but I am going to take any help you have to offer, and be mighty darned glad to get it.

"And now you want to see Helen Monteith?"

Mason nodded.

"All right," the sheriff said, "you'll have to come over to the jail, and only you can see her. You'll have to leave the others behind."

Mason entered the cement-floored office of the jail as Sheriff Barnes swung back the heavy iron door. The atmosphere was permeated with the sickly sweet odor of jail disinfectant, with the psychic emanations from scores of dispirited derelicts. It exerted a strangely depressing influence upon one who had not become immune to it.

"She's in the detention ward," the sheriff said, "and the detention ward's over on that side. The matron's the jailer's wife. I'll have to get her and bring her down. You can go in that room and wait."

Mason entered the little office and waited some five minutes before the jailer's wife escorted Helen Monteith into the room.

"Well," she said, as she dropped into a chair, "what do you want?"

"I want to help you, if I can," Mason told her.

"I'm afraid you can't. I seem to have put my foot in it all the way along the line."

The matron said, "I'll stand just outside the door here, and . . ."

"Go ahead and close the door," the sheriff told her. "Let them talk in private."

When the door had swung shut Mason said, "Tell me about it."

Helen Monteith seemed fatigued to the point of spiritual and mental exhaustion. "Oh, what's the use," she said. ". . . I guess I was just too happy, that's all . . . The bottom dropped out of everything. By the time this is over, my job will be gone. The only man I ever really loved is dead. They're accusing me of murdering him, and . . . and . . ." She blinked back tears and said, "No, I'm not going to cry. It's all right. When a woman reaches my age, crying is just a sign of self-sympathy, and I don't intend to give in to myself."

"Why did you leave Della Street?" Mason asked.

"Because," she said, in that same dispirited tone of voice, "I wanted to go back and burn the letters I'd received from . . . *from my husband,*" she said, with a trace of defiance in her voice.

Mason said, "He may really have been your legal husband, after all. There's some doubt as to the validity of his marriage to Helen Watkins. If you'll help, we may be able to do something."

"There's nothing you can do," she said wearily. "They have the cards all stacked against me. I didn't tell you the worst thing against me."

"What?" Mason asked.

"I went up to that mountain cabin Tuesday, the sixth."

"Why?" Mason asked.

"Just sentiment," she said. "No one will believe me, no one would ever understand. I suppose you'd have to be in love to get my viewpoint anyway, and probably it has to be a love which comes after you've had one complete and utter disillusionment. Anyway, I went up there just because I'd been so happy there. I just wanted to go up and bask in the smell of the woods, in the sunshine and the aura of peace and tranquillity which surrounds the place. The chipmunks were so friendly, the bluejays so impudently inquisitive . . . I wanted to live over in my mind the happiness I'd had."

"Why didn't you tell that to the officers?"

"I just didn't want to be made to appear ridiculous. It's the same thing you have to contend with in love letters. They seem sacred and tender when you read them, but when they are read in court, they sound simply ghastly."

"Someone saw you up there?"

"Yes, I was arrested for speeding. That is, the traffic officer says I was speeding. Personally, I think he just wanted to round out his day's quota of arrests. It was a steep curve, and he claimed there was a limit of fifteen miles, and I was going twenty-five . . . Anyway, he took the number of my car, and gave me a traffic ticket to sign, and I signed it. They found out about that, and that puts me on the spot."

"And how about the gun?" Mason asked.

"My husband asked me to get that gun for him."

"Did he say why?"

"No. He rang me up at the library and asked me if there wasn't a gun in the collection which would shoot. I told him I didn't know, but I supposed so. He said he'd seen a derringer in there, which he thought was in pretty good shape, and thought we could get shells for it. He asked me to get the gun and get some shells for it. He said he only wanted it for a few days, and then I could put it back."

"Didn't that request seem rather unreasonable?" Mason asked.

"Of course not. I was in love," she said simply, as one might talk of a happy home life before it had been completely destroyed by some catastrophe.

"So you went back home in order to burn up the letters?"

"Yes."

"Wasn't it to hide the shells?"

"No."

"But you did try to hide the shells?"

"After I got there, I decided it would be a good plan to get rid of them."

"And the parrot?" Mason asked. "Did you kill the parrot?"

"Good heavens, no! Why should I want to kill the parrot?"

"You probably noticed," Mason said, "that the parrot kept repeating, 'Put down that gun, Helen . . . don't shoot . . . My God, you've shot me.' "

"Well, you can't blame that on me," she said. "My husband purchased that parrot at a pet store on Friday the second. I'm not responsible for anything a parrot says. What's more, that parrot never was anywhere near that cabin."

Sudden tears flooded her eyes. "I can't believe, I simply *can't* believe that he ever intended to do anything which wasn't for my complete happiness. Oh, God, *why* did he have to die. He was so gentle and kind and considerate and had such a wonderful character."

Mason crossed over to her and placed his hand on her shoulder. "Take it easy," he said, "save your nerves as much as you can. You're going through an ordeal tonight before the coroner's jury."

"What do you want me to do?" she asked, choking back sobs. "T-t-tell them I refuse to answer questions? I understand that's what the b-b-best lawyers tell c-c-clients who are accused of m-m-murder."

Mason said, "On the contrary, you're going to go on that witness stand and answer all their questions. No matter how they hurl accusations at you, or how they try to browbeat you, you're going to keep your head and simply tell the truth. It's going to be an ordeal, but you're going to emerge with flying colors."

"That isn't the attitude you adopted last night," she said. "Then you were trying to keep me away from the police."

"Not the police," Mason said. "I was trying to keep you away from a parrot killer."

"What do you mean?"

"I thought," Mason said, "that it was well within the bounds of possibility that someone would try to kill the parrot at your house. If you were there and heard the intruder . . . Well, whoever killed that parrot had already committed one murder. One more or less wouldn't have made a great deal of difference."

"But how did you know someone was going to try and kill the parrot?"

"It was just a hunch," Mason said. ". . . Think you can go through with it tonight?"

"I'll try," she promised.

"All right," Mason told her. "Let's cheer up; let's get this feeling of hopelessness completely licked."

"I'll try to stick out my chin and take it," she told him. "Just a few days ago I thought I was the happiest woman in the world. Now, if I dared to let myself start sympathizing with myself, I'd feel I was the most miserable. It's quite a comedown."

"I know it is," Mason sympathized.

"I've lost the man I loved, and I'm accused of murder on top of that."

"That accusation isn't going to last very long," Mason said.

She managed to smile, tilted her chin up a bit. "All right, let's go."

CHAPTER TWELVE

ANDY TEMPLET, the coroner, having acquired some reputation as a practical philosopher, refused to be stampeded by the flattering preparations which the press had made for reporting the inquest. He stood calmly and at ease while press photographers snapped pictures of his kindly, twinkling eyes and the whimsical smile about his mouth. Having called the inquest to order and selected his jury, he made a brief speech in which there was no attempt at grandiose eloquence.

"Now, folks," he said, "we've got to determine the cause of death in this case. In other words, we've got to find out how this man died. And if somebody killed him, and we know who that someone was, we can say so. If we don't know, we hadn't better try to fix the responsibility. We aren't here to try anyone for anything. We're just trying to determine how Fremont C. Sabin met his death, up in his mountain cabin.

"Now, the coroner has charge of inquests. Most of the time he lets the district attorney ask questions, when the district attorney wants to, but that doesn't mean the district attorney runs the inquest. It simply means the district attorney is here to help us, and, in a case of this kind, he's here to try and uncover facts which will help him convict the murderer. The sheriff is also an interested party, and the sheriff has a lawyer here, Mr. Perry Mason. Mr. Mason is representing the heirs—that is, one of the heirs. Mr. Mason wants to find out how the murder was committed. Mr. Mason is also representing Helen Monteith.

"I want everybody to understand that we ain't going to have any monkeyshines, and we ain't going to have any oratory, or long-winded objections. We're going to move right along with this thing, and if I get my order of proof all cockeyed, that's my responsibility. I don't want anybody to point out anything except facts. I don't want anybody to try and get the witnesses rattled.

"Now, I'm going to start out asking questions. When I get done I'll let the district attorney ask questions, and I'll let Perry Mason ask questions, and the jurors can ask questions. But let's get down to brass tacks and keep moving. Do you all understand?"

"I understand," Perry Mason said.

The district attorney said, "Of course, the coroner's idea of what is a technicality may differ from mine, in which event . . ."

". . . In which event," the coroner interrupted, "what *I think* is going to be what counts. I'm just a plain, common, ordinary citizen. I've tried to get a coroner's jury of plain, common, ordinary citizens. The object back of this proof is to give the coroner's jury a chance to figure what happened. We haven't got a jury of lawyers. We've got a jury of citizens. I think I know what they want. . . . Anyway, I know what *I* want."

Andy Templet stilled the titter which ran over the

courtroom and said, "I think we'd better have the neighbor who discovered the body, first."

Fred Waner came forward and was sworn. He gave his name, address, and occupation.

The coroner said, "You found the body, didn't you, Mr. Waner?"

"Yes."

"Where?"

"In his mountain cabin, up in Grizzly Flats."

"He owned a cabin up there?"

"Yes, that's right."

"Now, I've got some pictures here. We'll connect them up later, but they're pictures of the cabin. You take a look at them and tell me if that's the cabin."

"Yes, that's right. Those are pictures of the cabin."

"All right. You found the body there. When was it?"

"It was Sunday, September eleventh."

"About what time?"

"Around three or four o'clock in the afternoon."

"What happened?"

"Well, I was coming along the road, driving up to my place, and got to wondering whether Sabin had got in for the fishing. I hadn't seen him, but he usually managed to get in when they opened up the fishing in Grizzly Creek, so I stopped the car to take a look at the house, and heard the parrot screaming something awful. So I says to myself, 'Well, he's there if his parrot is there,' so I drove up to the house. The shutters were all down the way it is when the place is closed up, and the garage was closed and locked, and I thought, 'Shucks, I've made a mistake, there ain't anyone home.' So I started to drive away, and then I heard this parrot again."

"What was the parrot saying?" the coroner asked.

Waner grinned and said, "The parrot was cussing a blue streak; he wanted something to eat."

"So what did you do?"

"Well, I got to wondering if Sabin had maybe left the parrot there without being there himself. I figured maybe he'd gone fishing, but if he had, I didn't see why he'd pull all the shutters down; so I got out and looked around. Well, the garage was locked, but I could get the doors open a crack, just enough to see that Sabin's car was in there, so then I went around to the door and knocked, and didn't get any answer, and finally, thinking maybe something was wrong, pried open one of the shutters and looked inside. This parrot was screaming all the time, and, looking inside, I saw a man's hand lying on the floor. So then I got the window up and got inside. I saw right away that the man had been dead for quite a while. There was some food for the parrot on the floor, and a pan that had held water, but the water was all gone. I went right over to the telephone and telephoned you. I didn't touch anything."

"Then what did you do?"

"Then I got out into the fresh air, and left the place closed up until you got there," the witness said.

"I don't think there's any need to ask this man any more questions, is there?" the coroner asked.

The district attorney said, "I'd like to ask one question, just for the sake of fixing the jurisdictional fact. The body was that of Fremont C. Sabin?"

"Yes, it was pretty far gone, but it was Sabin, all right."

"How long have you known Fremont C. Sabin?"

"Five years."

"I think that's all," the district attorney said.

"Just one more question," the coroner said. "Nothing was touched until I got there, was it, Waner?"

"Absolutely nothing, except the telephone."

"And the sheriff came up there with me, didn't he?"

"Yes, that's right."

"Well, we'll hear from the sheriff," the coroner said.

Sheriff Barnes eased himself into the witness chair, crossed his legs, and settled back at his ease. "Now, Sheriff," the coroner said, "suppose you tell us just what you found when we went up there to Sabin's cabin."

"Well, the body was lying on the floor, on its left side. The left arm was stretched out, and the fingers clenched. The right arm was lying across the body. Things were pretty bad in there. We opened all the windows and got as much air in as we could . . . looking over the windows before we opened them, of course, to make certain they

130

were locked on the inside, and there weren't any evidences that they'd been tampered with.

"There was a spring lock on the door, and that lock was closed, so whoever did the killing, walked out and pulled the door 'shut behind him. We got the parrot back in the cage, and closed the cage. It had been propped open with a notched pine stick. I took some chalk and traced the position of the body on the floor, and traced the position of the gun, and then the coroner went through the clothes, and then we had a photographer take a few pictures of the body, as it was lying on the floor."

"You've got prints of those pictures with you?" the coroner asked.

"Yes, here they are," the sheriff said, and produced some photographs. The coroner, taking possession of them, said, "All right, I'll hand all these over to the jury a little later. Let's find out, now, what happened."

"Well, after we moved the body and got the place aired out," the sheriff said, "we started looking things over. I'll start with the kitchen. There was a garbage pail in the kitchen; in the garbage pail were the shells of two eggs, and some bacon rind, a piece of stale toast, badly burnt on one side, and a small can of pork and beans, which had been opened. On the gas stove—he had a pressure gas outfit up there—was a frying pan in which some pork and beans had been warmed up quite a while ago. The pan was all dry, and the beans had crusted all around the sides. There was still some coffee, and a lot of coffee grounds, in the pot on the stove. There was a knife and fork and a plate in the sink. There'd been beans eaten out of the plate. In the icebox was part of a roll of butter, a bottle of cream, and a couple of packages of cheese which hadn't been opened. There was a locker with a lot of canned goods, and a bread box, which had half a loaf of bread in it, and a bag with a couple of dozen assorted cookies.

"In the main room there was a table on which was a jointed fly rod, a book of flies, and a creel, in which was a mess of fish. Those fish had evidently been there about as long as the body. We made a box to put the creel in, got the box as nearly airtight as possible, and put the whole thing in and nailed it up, without touching the contents. Then we checked on the gun and found it was a forty-one caliber derringer, with discharged shells in each of the two barrels. The body had two bullet holes just below the heart, and, from the position of the bullet holes, we figured that both barrels of the gun had been fired at once.

"There were some rubber boots near the table, and there was dried mud on the boots; an alarm clock was on the table near the bed. It had stopped at two forty-seven; the alarm had been set for five-thirty; both the alarm and the clock had run down. The body was clothed in a pair of slacks, a shirt and sweater. There were wool socks and slippers on the feet.

"There was a telephone line running out of the cabin, and the next day, when Perry Mason and Sergeant Holcomb were helping me make an investigation, we found that the telephone line had been tapped. Whoever had done the tapping had established a headquarters in a cabin about three hundred and fifty yards from the Sabin cabin. It had evidently been an old, abandoned cabin, which had been fixed up and repaired when the wire-tapping apparatus was installed. We found evidences that whoever had been in the place had left hurriedly. There was a cigarette on the table, which had evidently been freshly lit, and then burnt down to ashes. The dust indicated that the place hadn't been used for a week or so."

"Did Helen Monteith make any statement to you about that gun?" the coroner asked.

"Yes, she did," the sheriff said. "That was only today."

"Now, just a moment," the district attorney inquired. "Was that statement made as a free and voluntary statement, and without any promises or inducements of any kind having been offered to her?"

"That's right," the sheriff said. "You asked her if she'd ever seen the gun before, and she said she had. She said she'd taken it at the request of her husband, and bought some shells for it; that she'd given him the gun and shells on Saturday, the third of September."

"Did she say who her husband was?" the district attorney inquired.

"Yes, she said the man she referred to as her husband was Fremont C. Sabin."

"Any questions anyone wants to ask of the sheriff?" the coroner inquired.

"No questions," Mason said.

"I think that's all for the moment," the district attorney said.

The coroner said, "I'm going to call Helen Monteith to the witness stand." He turned to the coroner's jury and said, "I don't suppose Mr. Mason will want his client to make any statement at this time. She'll probably decline to answer any questions, because she's being held in the detention ward on the suspicion of murder, but I'm going to at least get the records straight by letting you gentlemen take a look at her and hearing what she says when she refuses to answer."

Helen Monteith came forward, was sworn, and took the witness stand.

Mason said to the coroner, "Contrary to what you apparently expect, I am not advising Miss Monteith to refuse to answer questions. In fact, I am going to suggest that Miss Monteith turn to the jury and tell her story in her own way."

Helen Monteith faced the jury. There was extreme weariness in her manner, but also a certain defiance, and a certain pride. She told of the man who had entered the library, making her acquaintance, an acquaintance which ripened into friendship, and then into love. She told of their marriage; of the weekend honeymoon spent in the cabin in the mountains. Bit by bit she reconstructed the romance for the jury, and the shock which she had experienced when she had learned of the tragic aftermath.

Raymond Sprague fairly lunged at her, in his eagerness to cross-examine. "You took that gun from the museum exhibit?"

"Yes."

"Why did you do it?"

"My husband asked me for a gun."

"Why didn't you buy a gun?"

"He told me he needed one right away, and that, under the law, no store would deliver one for a period of three days after he'd ordered it."

"Did he say why he wanted the gun?"

"No."

"You knew it was stealing to take that gun?"

"I wasn't stealing it, I was borrowing it."

"Oh, Sabin promised to return it, did he?"

"Yes."

"And you want this jury to understand that Fremont C. Sabin deliberately asked you to steal the gun, with which he was killed, from a collection?"

Mason said, "Don't answer that, Miss Monteith. You just testify to facts. I think the jury will understand you, all right."

Sprague turned savagely to Mason and said, "I thought we weren't going to have any technicalities."

"We aren't," Mason assured him smilingly.

"That's a technical objection."

"It isn't an objection at all," Mason said. "It's simply an instruction to my client not to answer the question."

"I demand that she answer it," the district attorney said to the coroner.

The coroner said, "I think you can question Miss Monteith just about facts, Mr. Sprague. Don't ask her what she wants the jury to understand."

Sprague, flushing, said, "How about that parrot?"

"You mean Casanova?"

"Yes."

"Mr. Sabin bought it . . . that is, that's what I understood."

"When?"

"On Friday, the second of September."

"What did he say when he brought the parrot home?"

"Simply said that he'd always wanted a parrot, and that he'd bought one."

"And you kept that parrot with you after that?"

"Yes."

"Where were you on Sunday, the fourth of September?"

"I was with my husband."

"Where?"

"At Santa Delbarra."

"You registered in a hotel there?"

"Yes."

"Under what name?"

"As Mrs. George Wallman, of course."

"And Fremont C. Sabin was the George Wallman who was there with you?"

"Yes."

"And did he have this gun there at that time?"

"I guess so. I don't know. I didn't see it."

"Did he say anything about going up to this cabin for the opening of the fishing season?"

"Of course not. He was leading me to believe he was a poor man, looking for work. He told me that Monday was a holiday, but he had some people he wanted to see anyway—so I went home Monday."

"That was the fifth?"

"Yes."

"Where were you on Tuesday, the sixth?"

"I was in the library part of the day, and . . . and part of the day I drove up to the cabin."

"Oh, you were up at this cabin on Tuesday, the sixth?"

"Yes, that's what I said."

"And what did you do up there?"

"Simply drove around and looked at it."

"And what time was that?"

"About eleven o'clock in the morning."

"What was the condition of the cabin at the time?"

"It looked just like it had when I'd last left it."

"Were the shutters down?"

"Yes."

"Just the same as is shown in that photograph?"

"Yes."

"Did you hear a parrot?"

"No."

"The cabin seemed deserted?"

"Yes."

"Did you notice whether there was any car in the garage?"

"No."

"What did you do?"

"Just drove around there for a while, and then left."

"Why did you go up there?"

"I went up to . . . well, simply to see the place. I had some time off, and I wanted to take a drive, and I thought that was a nice drive."

"It was quite a long drive, wasn't it?"

"Yes."

"Now, you understand that the evidence points to the fact that Fremont C. Sabin was killed at approximately ten-thirty or eleven o'clock on the morning of September sixth?"

"Yes," she said.

"And that he arrived at the cabin on the afternoon of Monday, September fifth?"

"Yes."

"And did you want the coroner's jury to understand that you found the cabin with the shutters closed, saw no evidence of any occupancy, heard nothing of a parrot, and did not see Mr. Sabin at that time?"

"That's right. I found the cabin just as I have described, and I did not see Mr. Sabin. I had no idea he was there. I thought he was in Santa Delbarra, looking for a location for a grocery store."

Mason said, "I think this witness has given all the information which she has to impart. I think any further questions are in the nature of a cross-examination, and argumentative. There is no new information being elicited. I will advise the coroner and the district attorney that, unless some new phase of the case is gone into, I'm going to advise the witness not to answer any more questions."

"I'll open up a new phase of the case," the district attorney said threateningly. "Who killed that parrot which was kept in your house?"

"I don't know."

"This parrot was brought home to you on Friday, the second?"

"That's right."

"And on Saturday, the third, you left with your husband?"

"No, my husband left on Saturday afternoon and went to Santa Delbarra. Monday was a holiday. I drove up to Santa Delbarra Sunday, and spent Sunday night and Monday morning with him in the hotel. I returned Monday night to San Molinas. My next-door neighbor, Mrs. Winters, had been keeping the parrot. I arrived too late in the evening to call for it. The next day, Tuesday, the sixth, I didn't have to be at the library until three o'clock in the afternoon. I wanted to be away from people. I got up early in the morning, and drove to the cabin, and returned in time to go directly to the library at three o'clock."

"Isn't it a fact," the district attorney persisted, "that you returned to your house at an early hour this morning for the purpose, among other things, of killing the parrot which was in the house, the parrot which your next-door neighbor, Mrs. Winters, had kept while you spent your so-called honeymoon with the person whom you have referred to as your husband, in this mountain cabin?"

"That is not a fact. I didn't even know the parrot was dead until the sheriff told me."

The district attorney said, "I think perhaps I can refresh your recollection upon this subject, Miss Monteith."

He turned and nodded to his deputy, a young man who was standing near the doorway. The deputy stepped outside long enough to pick up a bundle covered with cloth, then hurried down the aisle, past the rows of twisted-necked spectators, to deliver the bundle to Sprague.

District Attorney Sprague dramatically whipped away the cloth. A gasp sounded from the spectators as they saw what the cloth had concealed—a bloodstained parrot cage, on the floor of which lay the stiff body of a dead parrot, its head completely severed.

"That," the district attorney said dramatically, "is *your* handiwork, isn't it, Miss Monteith?"

She swayed slightly in the witness chair. "I feel giddy," she said. ". . . Please take that away . . . The blood . . ."

The district attorney turned to the spectators and announced triumphantly, "The killer quails when confronted with evidence of her . . ."

"She does no such thing," Mason roared, getting to his feet and striding belligerently toward Sprague. "This young woman has been subject to inhuman treatment. Within the short space of twenty-four hours, she has learned that the man whom she loved, and whom she regarded as her husband, was killed. No sympathy was offered her in her hour of bereavement. Instead of sympathy being extended, she was dragged out into the pitiless glare of publicity and . . ."

"Are you making a speech?" the district attorney interrupted.

Mason said, "No, I'm finishing yours."

"I'm perfectly capable of finishing my own," the district attorney shouted.

"You try to finish that speech *you* started," Mason told him, "and you'll . . ."

The coroner's gavel banged. The sheriff, jumping from his seat, came striding forward.

"We're going to have order," the coroner said.

"You can have it from me," Mason told him, "if you keep the district attorney from making speeches. The facts of the matter are that this young woman, who has been subjected to a nerve strain well calculated to make her hysterical, is suddenly confronted with a gruesome, gory spectacle. Her natural repugnance is interpreted by the district attorney as an indication of guilt. That's his privilege. But when he starts making a speech about it . . ."

"I didn't make a speech about it," the district attorney said.

"Well," the coroner observed, "we're going to have no more speeches made by either side. The coroner is inclined to feel that it's asking pretty much of any young woman to have a gruesome spectacle like this suddenly thrust in front of her."

"It was done," Mason said, "purely as a grandstand,

purely for the purpose of capitalizing on Miss Monteith's overwrought condition."

"I had no such intention," the district attorney said.

"What did you have in mind?" the coroner asked.

"I merely wanted to identify the parrot as being the one which had been given to her by her husband on Friday, September second."

"He can do that," Mason said, "without throwing all this blood-stained paraphernalia in her lap."

"I don't need any suggestions from you," Sprague said.

The sheriff stepped forward. "If the coroner wants to make any rulings," he said drily, "I'm here to enforce them."

"The coroner is going to make a ruling," Andy Templet announced. "The coroner is going to rule that there'll be no more personalities exchanged between counsel. The coroner's also going to rule that there'll be no more sudden and dramatic production of blood-stained garments, bird cages, or dead birds."

"But I only wanted to identify the parrot," the district attorney insisted.

"I heard you the first time," the coroner told him, "and I hope you heard the coroner. Now, let's proceed with the inquest."

"That's all," the diistrict attorney said.

"May I ask a question?" Mason inquired.

The coroner nodded assent.

Mason stepped forward and said in a low, kindly voice, "I don't wish to subject your nerves to any undue strain, Miss Monteith, but I'm going to ask you to try and bring yourself to look at this parrot. I'm going to ask you to study it carefully, and I'm going to ask you whether this *is* the parrot which your husband brought home to you."

Helen Monteith made an effort at self-control. She turned and looked down at the lifeless parrot in the cage, then quickly averted her head. "I c-c-can't," she said, in a quavering voice, "but the parrot my husband brought home had one claw missing. I think it was from his right foot. My husband said he'd caught the foot in a rat trap, and . . ."

"This parrot has no claws missing," Mason said.

"Then it isn't the same parrot."

"Just a moment," Mason said; "I'm going to ask you to make another identification."

He nodded a signal to Paul Drake, who, in turn, passed the word to an operative who was waiting in the corridor. The operative came through the door carrying a caged parrot.

Amid a silence so tense that the steps of the detective could be heard as he walked down the carpeted aisle, the caged parrot suddenly broke into shrill laughter.

Helen Monteith's lips quivered. Apparently she was restraining herself from hysteria by a supreme effort.

Mason took the caged parrot from the operative. "Hush, Polly," he said.

The parrot twisted its head first to one side, then the other, leered about him at the courtroom with twinkling, wicked little eyes; then, as Mason set the cage on the table, the bird hooked its beak on the cross-wires of the cage, and completely circled it, walking over the top, head downward, to return to the perch as though proud of the accomplishment.

"Nice Polly," Mason said.

The parrot shuffled its feet on the perch.

Helen Monteith turned to regard the parrot. "Why," she said, "that's Casanova. . . . The sheriff told me he'd been killed."

The parrot, tucking its head slightly to one side, said in a low, throaty voice, "Come in and sit down, won't you? Come in and sit down, take that chair . . . *Squawk* . . . *Squawk* . . . Put down that gun, Helen . . . don't shoot . . . *Squawk* . . . *Squawk* . . . My God, you've shot me."

The spectators stared wide-eyed at the drama of the parrot apparently accusing the witness.

"That's Casanova!" Helen Monteith exclaimed.

The district attorney said dramatically, "I want the words of this parrot in the record. The parrot is accusing the witness. I want the record to show it."

Mason regarded the district attorney with a half smile twisting his lips. "Do I understand," he inquired, "that you're adopting this parrot as your witness?"

"The parrot has made a statement. I want it in the record," the district attorney insisted.

"But the parrot hasn't been sworn as a witness," Mason observed.

The district attorney appealed to the coroner. "The parrot has made a statement. It was a plainly audible statement."

"I would like to know," Mason said, "whether the district attorney is making the parrot his witness."

"I'm not talking about witnesses," Sprague countered. "I'm talking about parrots. This parrot made a statement. I want it in the record."

"If the parrot is to be a witness," Mason said, "I should have *some* right of cross-examination."

"Well," the coroner ruled, "a parrot can't be a witness, but the parrot *did* say something. What those words were can be put in the record for what they're worth. I think the coroner's jury understands the situation thoroughly. I never did believe in putting things in a record and then striking them out. When jurors hear things, they've heard them, and that's that. Now, go on with the inquest."

"I think that's all the questions I have," Mason said.

"That's all," Sprague said, "except . . . wait a minute. . . . Miss Monteith, if this parrot is Casanova, then where did the parrot come from that was killed?"

"I don't know," she said.

"It was in your house."

"I can't help that."

"You must have had something to do with it."

"I didn't."

"But you're certain this is Casanova?"

"Yes. I can identify him by that claw that's missing, and by what he said about dropping the gun."

"Oh, you've heard *that* before, have you?"

"Yes. My husband commented on it when he brought the bird home with him."

The district attorney said, "Miss Monteith, I'm not satisfied that your violent emotional reaction when this dead parrot was brought before you is purely the result of a nervous condition. Now, I'm going to insist that you look closely at this parrot and . . ."

Mason got to his feet and said, "You don't need to look at that parrot, Miss Monteith."

Sprague flushed and said, "I insist that she does."

"And I insist that she doesn't," Mason said. "Miss Monteith is not going to answer any more questions. She's been a witness. She's under a great emotional strain. I think the jury will understand my position as her attorney in announcing that she has now completed her testimony. She has given the district attorney and the coroner an opportunity to ask her all reasonable questions. I am not going to have the examination unduly prolonged."

"He can't do that," Sprague said to the coroner.

"I've already done it," Mason told him.

The coroner said, "I don't know whether he can or not, but I know that this young woman is nervous. I don't think you're making proper allowance for that condition, Sprague. Under ordinary circumstances, a widow is given condolences and sympathy. She's particularly spared from any nerve shock. This witness certainly has been subjected to a series of trying experiences during the last twenty-four hours. As far as the coroner is concerned, she's going to be excused. We're trying to complete this inquest at one sitting. I'm getting facts, that's all. And I want to keep moving. You'll have plenty of opportunity to ask her questions before the Grand Jury, and on the witness stand . . . I'm going to ask Mrs. Helen Watkins Sabin to come forward as a witness."

"She ain't here," the sheriff said.

"Where is she?"

"I don't know, I haven't been able to serve a subpoena on her."

"How about Steven Watkins?"

"The same with him."

"Is Waid here, the secretary?"

"Yes. He's been subpoenaed and is here."

"Well, let's hear from Sergeant Holcomb," the coroner said. "Sergeant Holcomb, come forward and be sworn, please."

Sergeant Holcomb took the witness stand. The coroner said, "Now, you're a sergeant on the homicide squad of the Metropolitan Police, aren't you, Sergeant, and you know all about the investigation of murder cases, and the scientific method of apprehending criminals?"

"That's right," Sergeant Holcomb admitted.

"Now you got this box with the creel of fish in it, that Sheriff Barnes sent in?"

"Yes, that was received at the technical laboratory of the police department. We had previously received a telephone call from Sheriff Barnes about it."

"What did you find out about the fish?" the coroner asked.

"We made some tests," Sergeant Holcomb said. "I didn't make the tests myself, but I was present when they were made, and know what the experts found."

"What did they find?"

"They found that there had been a limit of fish in the creel; that the fish were, of course, badly decomposed, but, as nearly as could be ascertained, the fish had been cleaned and wrapped in willow leaves. They had not been washed after being wrapped in willow leaves."

"And you went up to the cabin with Sheriff Barnes the next day?"

"That's right. Sheriff Barnes wanted me to see the cabin, and we were to meet Richard Waid there. He was coming on from New York by plane, and we wanted to meet him in a place where our first conversation wouldn't be interrupted by newspaper reporters."

"All right, go on," the coroner said.

"Well," Holcomb observed, "we went to the cabin. We met Mr. Mason on the road up to the cabin. Richard Waid came while we were there at the cabin."

"What did you find at the cabin, in the line of physical conditions?" the coroner asked.

"Just about the same as has been described."

"At this time," the coroner said, "I think the jury had better take a look at all of these photographs, because I'm going to ask Sergeant Holcomb some questions about them."

The coroner waited while the photographs were passed around to the jurors, then turned back to Sergeant Holcomb.

"Sergeant Holcomb," he said, "I want to give the

members of this jury the benefit of your experience. I want you to tell them what the various things in that cabin indicate."

The coroner glanced down at Perry Mason and said, "I suppose you may object that this is a conclusion of the witness, but it seems to me this man has had a lot of experience, and I don't know why he shouldn't . . ."

"Not at all," Mason said. "I think it's a very wise question. I think it's a perfectly proper way of getting at the ultimate facts of the case."

Sergeant Holcomb shifted himself to an easier position in the witness chair, gazed impressively at the jury, and said, "Helen Monteith killed Fremont C. Sabin. There are dozens of things which would be sufficient to establish an absolutely ironclad case against her, before any jury. First, she had motive. Sabin had married her under an assumed name; he had placed her in the position of being a bigamous wife. He had lied to her, tricked her, and deceived her. When she found out that the man she had married was Fremont C. Sabin, and that Sabin had a wife very much alive at the moment, she shot him. She probably didn't intend to shoot him when she went to the cabin. Our experience has been that, in emotional murders of this nature, a woman frequently takes a gun for the purpose of threatening a man, for the purpose of frightening him, or for the purpose of making him believe that she isn't to be trifled with; then, having pointed the gun at him, it's a simple matter to pull the trigger, an almost unconscious reflex, a momentary surrender to emotion. The effects, of course, are disastrous.

"Second, Helen Monteith had the murder weapon in her possession. Her statement that she gave it to her husband is, of course, absurd on the face of it. The crime could not have been suicide. The man didn't move from the time he fell to the floor. The gun was found some distance away, and was *wiped clean of fingerprints*.

"Third, she admits having been present at the cabin at the exact moment Sabin was murdered. She, therefore, combines motive, means and opportunity."

"How do you fix that exact moment of the murder?" the coroner asked.

"It's a matter of making correct deductions from circumstantial evidence," Sergeant Holcomb said.

"Just a minute," Mason interrupted. "Wouldn't it be better to let the sergeant tell the jury the various factors which control the time element in this case, and let the jurors judge for themselves?"

"I don't know," the coroner admitted. "I'm trying to expedite matters as much as possible."

Sergeant Holcomb said, "It would be absolutely foolish to resort to any such procedure. The interpretation of circumstantial evidence is something which calls for a highly specialized training. There are some things from which even the layman can make logical deductions, but on a complicated matter it requires years of experience. I have had that experience, and I am properly qualified to interpret the evidence for the jury. Therefore, I say that Fremont C. Sabin met his death sometime between ten o'clock in the morning and around noon, on Tuesday, the sixth day of September."

"Now, just explain to the jury how you interpret the evidence so as to fix the time," the coroner said.

"First, we go back to known facts, and reason from them," Sergeant Holcomb said. "We know that Fremont C. Sabin intended to go to his cabin on Monday, the fifth, in order to take advantage of the opening of fishing season on the sixth. We know that he actually did go there; we know that he was alive at ten o'clock in the evening of the fifth, because he talked with his secretary on the telephone. We know that he went to bed, that he wound the alarm clock and set the alarm. We know that the alarm went off at five-thirty. We know that he arose, went out, and caught a limit of fish. It is problematical how long it would take him to catch a limit, but, in discussing fishing conditions with other anglers on the creek, it would seem that with the utmost good fortune he could not possibly have caught a limit before nine-thirty o'clock. He returned to the cabin, then, at between ten and eleven in the morning. He had already had a breakfast, two eggs, probably scrambled, some bacon and some coffee. He was once more hungry. He opened a can of beans, warmed those up and ate them. He did this before he even bothered to put his fish in the icebox. He left his fish in the creel, intending to put them in the icebox as soon as he had washed them. But he was hungry enough to want to finish with his lunch before he put the fish away. In the ordinary course of things, he would have put those fish away immediately after he had eaten, probably before he had even washed his dishes. He didn't do that."

"Why don't you place the time as being later than noon?" the coroner asked.

"Those are the little things," Sergeant Holcomb said, with very evident pride, "which a trained investigator notices, and which others don't. Now, the body was clothed in a light sweater and slacks. From the observations which I made on the temperature in that cabin, I found that it varies quite sharply. The shade is such that the sun doesn't get on the roof good until after eleven o'clock. Thereafter it heats up very rapidly until about four o'clock, when once more shade strikes the roof, and it cools off quite rapidly thereafter, becoming cold at night.

"Now, there was a fire laid in the fireplace. That fire hadn't been lit, which shows that it wasn't late enough in the evening for it to have become cold. From noon until around four in the afternoon, it would have been too hot for a person to have been comfortable in a sweater. The records show that the fifth, sixth and seventh were three very warm days—that is, it was warm during the daytime. Up there at that elevation it cooled off quite rapidly at night. It was necessary to have a fire in the evening, in order to keep from being uncomfortably cool. That cabin, you understand, is just a mountain cabin, rather light in construction, and not insulated against conditions of temperature, as a house in the city would be."

"I see," the coroner remarked approvingly. "Then you feel that Mr. Sabin must have returned and had his second breakfast—or lunch—before the sun got on the roof?"

"That's right."

"I think that covers the situation very comprehensively," the coroner said.

"May I ask a question or two?" Mason inquired.

"Certainly."

"How do you know," Mason asked, "that Mr. Sabin didn't meet his death, say, for instance, on Wednesday, the seventh, instead of on the sixth?"

"Partially, from the condition of the body," Sergeant Holcomb said. "The body had been there at least six days. Probably, seven. In the heat and closeness of the room, decomposition had been quite rapid. Moreover, there's another reason. The decedent had had a breakfast of bacon and eggs. Mr. Sabin was an enthusiastic fisherman. He went up to the cabin for the purpose of being there on the opening morning of fishing season. It is inconceivable that he would have gone fishing on that first morning and not caught at least *some* fish. If he had caught them, there would have been evidences that he'd eaten them for breakfast the next morning instead of bacon and eggs. There were no remains of fish anywhere in the garbage pail, nor in the garbage pit in the back of the house, to which the contents of the garbage pail were transferred each day."

And Sergeant Holcomb smiled at the jury, as much as to say, "That shows how easy it is to avoid a lawyer's trap."

"Very well," Mason said, "Let's look at it from another angle. The fire was laid in the fireplace, but hadn't been lit, is that right?"

"Yes."

"Now, it's rather chilly there in the mornings?"

"Quite chilly."

"And at night?"

"Yes."

"Now, according to your theory, the alarm went off at five-thirty, and Mr. Sabin got up to go fishing, is that right?"

"Yes."

"And cooked himself rather a sketchy breakfast?"

"A hasty breakfast, you could call it," Sergeant Holcomb said. "When a person gets up at five-thirty in the morning on the opening day of the season, he's anxious to get out and get the fish."

"I see," Mason said. "Now, when Mr. Sabin came back from his fishing trip, he was in very much of a hurry to get something to eat. We may assume that the first thing he did when he entered the house, and immediately after removing his boots, was to get himself something to eat. Next in order of importance would have been washing the fish and putting them in the icebox. Is that right?"

"That's right."

"Yet, according to your theory," Mason said, "after he got back, he took enough time to lay the fire in the fireplace, all ready for lighting, before he even took care of his fish."

Sergeant Holcomb's face clouded for a moment, then he said, "No, he must have done that the night before." Having thought a minute, he added, triumphantly, "Of course, he did it the night before. He didn't have any occasion for a fire in the morning: it was cold when he got up, but he went right out in the kitchen and cooked his breakfast, and then went out fishing."

"Exactly," Mason said. "But he had reason for a fire the night before, I believe."

"What do you mean?"

"In other words," Mason said, "we know that he was at the cabin at four o'clock on the afternoon of Monday, the fifth. We can surmise that he remained at the cabin until shortly before ten o'clock in the evening, when he went out to place a phone call. If it was cold Monday evening, why didn't he light a fire?"

"He did," Sergeant Holcomb said. "He must have. There's no evidence to show that he didn't."

"Exactly," Mason went on. "But when the body was found, a fresh fire was laid in the fireplace. Now, according to your theory, he either laid that fire Monday night, in a grate that had just been used—or else he laid it the next day, after he got back from fishing. That is, he took time to lay the fire before he even took care of his fish. Does that seem logical to you?"

Sergeant Holcomb hesitated a moment, then said, "Well, that's one of those little things. That doesn't cut so

148

much ice. Lots of times you'll find little things which are more or less inconsistent with the general interpretation of evidence."

"I see," Mason said. "And when you encounter such little things, what do you do, Sergeant?"

"You just ignore 'em," Sergeant Holcomb said.

"And how many such little things have you ignored in reaching your conclusion that Fremont C. Sabin was murdered by Helen Monteith?"

"That's the only one," Sergeant Holcomb said.

"Very well, let's look at the evidence from a slightly different angle. Take the alarm clock, for instance. The alarm was run down, was it not?"

"Yes."

"And where was this alarm clock placed?"

"On the shelf by the bed—or rather on a little table by the bed."

"Quite close to the sleeper?"

"Yes."

"Within easy reaching distance?"

"Yes."

"And, by the way," Mason said, "the bed was made, is that right?"

"Yes."

"In other words, then, after getting up in the morning, at five-thirty, to go fishing, Mr. Sabin stopped long enough to lay a fire in the fireplace, long enough to make his bed, long enough to wash his breakfast dishes?"

Sergeant Holcomb said, "Well, it wouldn't take a man so very long to make his bed."

"By the way," Mason inquired, "did you notice whether there were clean sheets on the bed?"

"Yes, there were."

"Then, he not only must have made the bed, but must have changed the sheets. Did you find the soiled linen anywhere in the cabin, Sergeant?"

"I don't remember," Sergeant Holcomb said.

"There are no laundry facilities there. The soiled laundry is taken down in Mr. Sabin's car and laundered in the city, and returned to the cabin from time to time?"

"I believe that's right, yes."

"Then what became of the soiled sheets?" Mason asked.

"I don't know," Sergeant Holcomb said irritably. "You can't always connect up all these little things."

"Exactly," Mason said. "Now, let's get back to the alarm clock, Sergeant. The alarm was entirely run down?"

"That's right."

"The clock had a shut-off on it, by which the alarm could be shut off while it was sounding?"

"Yes, of course, all good clocks have that."

"Yes; and this was a good clock?"

"Yes."

"Yet the alarm had not been shut off?"

"I didn't notice . . . well, no, I guess not. It was completely run down."

"Yes," Mason said. "Now, is it your experience, Sergeant, as an expert interpreter of circumstantial evidence, that a sleeper permits an alarm to run entirely down before shutting it off?"

"Some people sleep more soundly than others," Sergeant Holcomb said.

"Exactly," Mason agreed, "but when a man is aroused by an alarm clock, his first natural reflex is to turn off the alarm—that is, if the alarm is within reaching distance, isn't that right?"

"Well, you can't always figure that way," Sergeant Holcomb said, his face slowly darkening in color. "Some people go back to sleep after they shut off an alarm, so they deliberately put the alarm clock where they can't get at it."

"I understand that," Mason said, "but in this case the alarm was placed within easy reach of the sleeper, apparently for the purpose of enabling the sleeper to shut off the alarm clock just as soon as it had wakened him, isn't that right?"

"Yes, I guess so."

"But that wasn't done?"

"Well, some persons sleep sounder than others."

"You mean that he wasn't wakened until after the alarm had run down?"

"Yes."

"But *after* an alarm runs down, it ceases to make any sound, does it not, Sergeant?"

"Oh, all that stuff isn't getting you anywhere," Sergeant Holcomb said. "The alarm was run down. He certainly got up. He didn't lie there and sleep, did he? He got up and went out and caught a limit of fish. Maybe the alarm ran down and didn't wake him up, and he woke up half an hour later, with a start, realizing that he'd overslept."

"And then," Mason said with a smile, "despite that realization, he paused to get himself breakfast, washed the breakfast dishes, made the bed, changed the sheets on the bed, laid the fire in the fireplace, and took the soiled bedclothes in his car down to the city to be laundered. Then he drove back to go fishing."

Sergeant Holcomb said, "All that stuff is absurd."

"*Why* is it absurd?" Mason asked.

Sergeant Holcomb sat in seething silence.

Mason said, "Well, Sergeant, since you seem to be unable to answer that question, let's get back to the alarm clock. As I remember it, you made some experiments with similar alarm clocks, didn't you, to find out how long it would take them to run down?"

"We made experiments with that same alarm clock," the sergeant said. "We made experiments with other alarm clocks and we wired the manufacturer."

"What did you find out?" Mason asked.

"According to the manufacturer, the alarm clocks would run down thirty to thirty-six hours after they'd been completely wound. According to an experiment we made with that clock, it ran down in thirty-two hours and twenty minutes after it was wound."

"In that case," Mason said, "the alarm clock must have been wound about twenty minutes after six o'clock, is that right?"

"Well, what's wrong with that?"

"Nothing," Mason said. "I'm simply asking you to interpret the evidence for the benefit of the jury, which is the thing you set out to do, Sergeant."

"Well, all right, then the clock was wound at twenty minutes past six. What of it?"

"Would you say at twenty minutes past six in the morning, or at twenty minutes past six in the evening?" Mason asked.

"In the evening," Sergeant Holcomb said. "The alarm went off at five-thirty. He wouldn't have wound the alarm clock in the morning, and if he had, he'd have wound up the alarm again. It was wound up at six-twenty in the evening."

"That's fine," Mason said, "that's exactly the point I'm making, Sergeant. Now, you have examined the long distance telephone bills covering calls which were put in from that cabin?"

"I have."

"And you found, did you not, that the last call listed was one which was placed at four o'clock in the afternoon, on Monday, the fifth of September, to Randolph Bolding, examiner of questioned documents?"

"That's right."

"And you talked with Mr. Bolding about that call?"

"Yes."

"Did Mr. Bolding know Mr. Sabin personally?"

"Yes."

"And did you ask him whether he recognized Mr. Sabin's voice?"

"Yes, I did. He knew it was Sabin with whom he was talking. He'd done some work for Sabin before."

"And Sabin asked him about some conclusions he had reached on some checks which had been given him?"

"Yes."

"And Bolding told him that, of course, the checks were forgeries; that he hadn't yet decided whether the endorsements on the back were in the same handwriting as the specimen which had been furnished him. And didn't he say he was inclined to think they were not?"

"Yes, I gathered that."

"And what else did Mr. Sabin say?"

"Mr. Sabin said he was going to send him another envelope, containing half a dozen more specimens of handwriting from five or six different people."

"Was that envelope received by Mr. Bolding?"

"It was not."

"Therefore, Mr. Sabin never had an opportunity to mail that letter?"

"So it would seem."

"Now, let us return for the moment to the identity of the murderer. We now understand that Mr. Sabin suspected Steve Watkins of having forged checks in a very large amount. A handwriting expert was checking Watkins' handwriting. Now, if Watkins had been guilty, what's more natural than for him to have tried to silence Mr. Sabin's lips by murder?"

Sergeant Holcomb's lips curled in a sneer. "Simply because," he said, "Watkins has a perfect alibi. Watkins left in an airplane, in the presence of a reputable witness, shortly after ten o'clock on the night of Monday the fifth, for New York. Every moment of his time is accounted for."

"Exactly," Mason said, "*If* we act on the assumption that Fremont C. Sabin was murdered on Tuesday, the sixth, but the trouble with your reasoning, Sergeant, is that there is nothing to indicate he was not murdered on the fifth."

"On the fifth?" Sergeant Holcomb exclaimed. "Impossible. The fishing season didn't open until the sixth, and Fremont Sabin would never have fished before the season opened."

"No," Mason said, "I daresay he wouldn't. I believe it's a misdemeanor, isn't it, Sergeant?"

"Yes."

"And murder is a felony?"

Sergeant Holcomb disdained to answer the question.

"Therefore," Mason said, "a murderer would have no conscientious scruples whatever against catching a limit of fish on the day before the season opened. Now, Sergeant, can you kindly tell the coroner, and this jury, what there is about your reasoning any stronger than a string of fish?"

Sergeant Holcomb stared at Perry Mason with startled eyes.

"In other words," Mason said, "having arrived at the

153

conclusion Helen Monteith murdered Fremont C. Sabin at eleven o'clock in the morning, on Tuesday, the sixth of September, you have interpreted all the evidence on the premises to support your conclusions; but a fair and impartial appraisement indicates that Fremont C. Sabin was murdered sometime around four o'clock in the afternoon of Monday, September the fifth, and that the murderer, knowing that it would be some time before the body was discovered, took steps to throw the police off the track and manufacture a perfect alibi by the simple expedient of going down to the stream, catching a limit of fish, the afternoon before the season opened, and leaving those fish in the creel.

"And in order to justify that conclusion, Sergeant, you don't have to disregard any 'insignificant' details. In other words, there were fresh sheets on the bed, because the bed had not been slept in. The alarm clock ran down at two forty-seven because the murderer left the cabin at approximately six-twenty o'clock in the afternoon, at which time he wound the alarm clock, after having carefully planted all the other bits of evidence. The reason the alarm which went off at five-thirty the next morning wasn't shut off is because the only occupant of that cabin was dead. And the reason the murderer was so solicitous about the welfare of the parrot was that he wanted the parrot to perjure itself by reciting the lines which the murderer had been at some pains to teach it—'Put down that gun, Helen . . . don't shoot. . . . My God, you've shot me.' The fire was laid in the fireplace because Sabin hadn't had reason to light it that afternoon. He was wearing a sweater because the sun had just got off the roof and it was cooling off, but he was murdered before it had become cool enough to light the fire.

"Sabin let the murderer in, because the murderer was someone whom he knew, yet Sabin had reason to believe he was in some danger. He had secured a gun from his wife, in order to protect himself. The murderer also had a gun which he intended to use, but after he entered the cabin he saw this derringer lying on the table near the bed, and he immediately realized the advantage of killing

Sabin with that gun rather than with the one he'd brought. The murderer had only to pick it up and shoot. Now then, Sergeant, will you kindly tell me what is wrong with that theory? Will you kindly interpret *any* of the evidence to indicate that it is erroneous, and will you please explain to the jury why your whole fine-spun thread of accusation depends on nothing stronger than a string of fish?"

Sergeant Holcomb squirmed uncomfortably in his chair, then blurted out, "Well, I don't believe Steve Watkins did it. That's just an out you've thought of to protect Helen Monteith."

"But what's wrong with that theory?" Mason asked.

"Everything," Sergeant Holcomb asserted.

"Point out one single inconsistency between it and the known facts."

Sergeant Holcomb suddenly started to laugh. "How," he demanded, "could Sabin have been killed at four o'clock in the *afternoon* of Monday, the fifth of September, and yet call his secretary on the long distance telephone, at ten o'clock in the *evening* of the fifth, and tell him everything was okay?"

"He couldn't," Mason admitted, "for the very good reason that he didn't."

"Well, that shoots your theory full of holes," Sergeant Holcomb announced triumphantly. ". . . Er . . . that is . . ."

"Exactly," Mason said; "as you have so suddenly realized, Sergeant, Richard Waid is the murderer."

Sheriff Barnes jumped to his feet. "Where's Richard Waid?" he asked.

The spectators exchanged blank glances. Two of the people near the door said, "If he was that young chap who was sitting in this chair, he got up and went out about two minutes ago."

The coroner said suddenly, "I'm going to adjourn this inquest for half an hour."

A hubbub of excited voices filled the room where the inquest was being held; chairs overturned as those nearest the door went rushing out pell-mell to the sidewalk. Sheriff Barnes, calling to one of his deputies, said, "Get on the teletype, watch every road out of town, get the city police to call all cars."

Mason turned to Helen Monteith and grinned. "That," he said, "I fancy, will be about all."

CHAPTER THIRTEEN

MASON sat in Sheriff Barnes' office, waiting patiently for the formalities incident to the release of Helen Monteith, who sat, as one in a daze, in a chair by the door.

Sheriff Barnes, pausing intermittently to check on telephone reports which were pouring in, tried to readjust the situation in his mind, through questions which he asked of Mason.

"I don't see yet just how you figured it," he said.

"Very simple," Mason told him. "The murderer must have been someone who had access to the parrot, someone who had planned the murder for a long time; someone who intended to pin the crime on Helen Watkins Sabin, since he probably knew nothing of Helen Monteith. Since he knew Sabin usually took the parrot with him when he went to the cabin on the opening of the fishing season, this person, who must have been someone residing in the house, started in educating the parrot to say, 'Drop that gun, Helen . . . don't shoot. . . . My God, you've shot me!' The whole crime had been carefully planned. Sabin was due to appear on Monday, the fifth, pick up the parrot, and go to the cabin for his fishing. The murderer had his plans all arranged, even to his manufactured alibi.

"And then, Sabin upset plans somewhat by appearing on the second and picking up the parrot. Taking the parrot with him, he heard the bird suddenly spring his new lines—'Drop that gun, Helen . . . don't shoot. . . . My God, you've shot me!'

"Probably no one will ever know just what happened after that, but Sabin either felt that his life was in danger, or else Casanova's repeated statements got on his nerves. He wanted to have a parrot around him, either because he liked parrots, or because in some way he wanted to fool the potential murderer—and I'm frank to confess that this substitution of the parrots has me guessing, and I won't rest until I've found out—if I ever can—just what was back of it.

"This much we do know: Sabin became alarmed. He switched parrots and got Miss Monteith to get a gun for him. Despite those precautions, he was murdered. The murderer naturally assumed that the parrot in the cage was Casanova, and took excellent steps to see that it didn't die before Sabin's body was discovered.

"Sabin, in the meantime, thought that he was getting a divorce—that is, he thought his wife was getting one. He thought that he would soon be free to follow up the bigamous marriage ceremony in Mexico with a perfectly legal marriage ceremony elsewhere.

"Waid, lying in wait in the cabin, in which he had ensconced himself so that he could overhear all the telephone conversations which took place over Sabin's telephone, was waiting for the proper moment to strike."

"Why was he so anxious to hear the telephone conversations?" the sheriff inquired.

"Because the success of his entire plan depended upon leaving in an airplane with Steve Watkins, at such a time that it would apparently give him an alibi. The only excuse they had to do this was the appointment Sabin had made to pay over a hundred thousand dollars to his wife in New York. He knew that Sabin was in constant telephone communication with his wife in Reno. Therefore, he had to be certain that nothing went wrong.

"While he was listening on the telephone, he heard Sabin put in a call for Bolding, the examiner of questioned documents, realized suddenly that if Sabin sent Bolding the specimens of handwriting of all the persons with whom he'd had business dealings, those handwriting specimens would include some of his own; that the handwriting expert would break down the endorsements on the back of those forged checks, and brand him as a forger. He realized, suddenly, that whatever he was to do had to be done swiftly. I think he had intended to wait until eight o'clock before committing the murder. He had his string of fish already caught, the evidence all ready to plant. Then, that telephone call came through. He knew that he had to get to Sabin before those documents went into the mail, so he jumped up and ran out of the cabin without even pausing to pick up the cigarette he had laid down on the table when he heard the telephone call come through."

"Why didn't you tip us off so we could grab Waid?" the sheriff grumbled.

Mason said, "Because the evidence would be materially strengthened by having Waid become panic-stricken, and make a sudden disappearance. Flight, in itself, is an evidence of guilt. You can see that Waid was panic-stricken. As soon as he realized he had murdered the wrong parrot, he knew how deadly the evidence of the parrot would be, because it would prove conclusively that the parrot didn't learn his speech by hearing the excited last words of Fremont C. Sabin, but had been carefully coached to repeat those words by someone who had access to it; and Waid was the only one, outside of Fremont Sabin, and the son Charles, who had access to the parrot. You will note that Steve Watkins didn't live in the house, and Mrs. Sabin had been away for six weeks.

"Of all the persons who had a complete alibi, the parrot was the one who had the best. The parrot was not at the scene of the shooting. That was attested to by Mrs. Winters. Therefore, the parrot couldn't have learned his speech from hearing Sabin say those words. I felt it was quite possible that Sabin's murderer might be in the room last night when I disclosed the switch in parrots. Charles Sabin had known of it for some time. The information came as news to Mrs. Sabin, Steve and Waid—I saw to that. . . . So Waid decided the only thing for him to do was to kill the parrot. He didn't know that other persons had heard the parrot's comments. You see, that's the trouble with teaching a parrot something to say: you never can tell how often he'll say it, or when he'll say it.

"But Waid had all the breaks in one way. He hadn't intended to pin the crime on Helen Monteith. It's probable that he knew nothing of Helen Monteith. He had intended to pin the crime on Helen Watkins Sabin. Imagine his consternation when he found that Helen Watkins Sabin had an alibi; that she had been in court in Reno when the murder was supposed to have been committed. Then, he suddenly realized there was an excellent opportunity to pin the crime on Helen Monteith, but he had to get that parrot out of the way. And then his confidence suddenly returned when he learned that the decree of divorce had been forged, and that Mrs. Sabin didn't have an alibi after all.

"Once having placed the time of the murder accurately, and disregarding the evidence of the string of fish to which Sergeant Holcomb attached such great importance, it became obvious that Sabin was not alive at ten o'clock on the evening of Monday, the fifth. Therefore, Waid's statement that he had talked with Sabin over the telephone must have been false."

Helen Monteith said, "Well, I hope they hang him! He killed one of the best men who ever lived. You've no idea how unselfish and considerate Mr. Sabin was. He thought of everything, no detail was too small to escape him. Nothing which would go for my comfort was overlooked."

"I can readily appreciate that," Mason said soberly. "Everything that he did . . . Wait a minute . . ."

He stopped abruptly.

"What's the matter?" the sheriff asked.

Mason said excitedly, "That will! He really executed that after he'd married you. Yet he didn't make any provision in it for you. He provided for everyone else."

"Yes," she said.

"Why didn't he provide for you?" Mason asked.

"I don't know. He would have had some good reason. I didn't want money, anyway. I wanted him."

Mason said, "That's the angle to this case I can't understand. Fremont Sabin made his will at the time he was negotiating that property settlement with his wife."

"What's wrong with that?" Sheriff Barnes asked.

Mason said, "It just doesn't fit into the picture. He makes provision for every one of the objects of his affection, but he doesn't make any provision whatever for Helen Monteith."

"That was because he didn't have any reason to," the sheriff said. "He'd married her in Mexico, and he was going to marry her again, later on. We know now that the reason for all this was that he was waiting for Helen Watkins Sabin to get her divorce. Naturally, he didn't expect to die in the meantime."

Mason said, "No, that doesn't cover it. The businessman doesn't make his will because he *expects* to die, but to take effect when he *does* die. He covers every possible eventuality. Notice that the will specifically provided for the payment of money to Helen Watkins Sabin in the event he died before the divorce decree had been granted and the money paid. In other words, she, having made a good faith attempt to carry out the agreement, was to be protected, regardless of what might happen to Sabin. That shows his essential fairness. Yet, he made no provision for Helen Monteith."

Helen Monteith said, "I didn't want him to. I'm not dependent on him for anything. I'm making my own living. I . . ."

Suddenly Mason got to his feet and started pacing the floor. Once or twice he made little gestures with his fingers as though checking off points against some mental inventory he was taking. Abruptly he turned to Della Street. "Della," he said, "go get the car. Fill it up with oil and gas, and bring it down to the front door. We're going to take a ride."

He turned to Sheriff Barnes and said, "Sheriff, I'd consider it as a personal favor if you'd expedite all the formalities as much as possible. Cut all the red tape you can. I want to get Helen Monteith out of here at once."

The sheriff studied him from beneath leveled eyebrows. "You think she's in some danger here?" he asked.

Mason didn't answer the question. He turned to Helen Monteith. "Do you suppose," he said, "you could help me check one phase of your alibi?"

"What do you mean, Mr. Mason?"

Mason said, "I want you to do something which is going to be a nerve strain. I hate to inflict it upon you, but it's necessary. There's one point we want to establish, immediately."

"What?" she asked.

"I think I know the real reason for that original substitution of parrots," Mason said. "I remarked a while ago that we'd probably never know just what caused Sabin to make that switch. Now I think we can get the real reason. If what I suspect is true, there's an angle to this case so vitally important that . . . Do you think you could stand a drive to Santa Delbarra? Do you think you could point out to me the exact room in the hotel where you last saw your husband?"

"I could," she said, "but I don't understand why."

Mason shifted his eyes to meet the steady inquiry in those of Sheriff Barnes. "We've been talking quite a bit about becoming hypnotized by circumstantial evidence. After a person once gets a fixed belief, he interprets everything which happens in the light of that belief. It's a dangerous habit to get into, and I'm afraid I haven't been entirely innocent, myself. I've been so busy pointing out the trap to others that I've walked into one myself without noticing what I was doing."

Sheriff Barnes said, "I don't know what you're after, Mason, but we'll rush things through. I have the matron coming over with all the personal property taken from Miss Monteith. . . . Here she is now. Check this property and pay particular attention to the contents of your purse, Miss Monteith. Then, sign this receipt on the back of this manila envelope."

Helen Monteith had just finished signing the receipt when Della Street entered the room and nodded to Mason. "All ready, Chief," she said.

Mason shook hands with the sheriff. "I may give you a ring later on, Sheriff," he said. "In the meantime, thanks a lot."

He took Helen Monteith's arm, and, with Della Street on the other side, piloted her out into the fresh air of the warm night.

Twice while they were riding up the long stretch of moonlit road to Santa Delbarra, Helen Monteith tried to find out from Perry Mason what he expected to find at the end of their journey. In both instances Mason avoided the inquiry.

Finally, in response to a direct question, Mason said frankly, "I don't know. I do know that on one side of this case there's an inconsistency, a place where the loose threads fail to tie up. I want to investigate that and make certain. I'm going to need you to help me. I realize it's a strain on you, but I see no way of avoiding it."

Thereafter he drove in silence until the highway swung up over a hill to dip down into the outskirts of Santa Delbarra.

"Now," Mason said to Helen Monteith, "if you'll tell me how to get to the hotel where you stayed . . ."

"It's not particularly inviting," she said. "It's inexpensive and . . ."

"I understand all that," Mason told her. "Just tell me how to get there."

"Straight down this street until I tell you to turn," she said.

Mason piloted the car down an avenue lined with palm trees silhouetted against the moonlit sky, until Helen Monteith said, "Here's the place. Turn to the right."

He swung the car to the right.

"Go two blocks, and the hotel is on the left-hand corner," she said.

Mason found the hotel, slid the car to a stop, and asked Helen Monteith, "Do you remember the room number?"

"It was room 29," she said.

Mason nodded to Della Street. "I want to go up to that room, Della," he said. "Go to the room clerk, ask him if the room is occupied. If it is, find out who's in it."

As Della Street vanished through the door to the lobby, Mason locked his car, and took Helen Monteith's arm. They entered the hotel. "An elevator?" Mason asked.

"No," she said. "You walk up."

Della Street turned away from the desk and walked toward Mason. Her eyes were wide with startled astonishment. "Chief," she said, "I . . ."

"Let's wait," Mason warned her.

They climbed the creaky stairs to the third floor,

walked down the long corridor, its thin carpet barely muffling the echoing sound of their footfalls.

"This is the door," Helen Monteith said.

"I know," Mason told her. "The room's rented . . . isn't it, Della?"

She nodded wordless assent, and Mason needed only to study the tense lines of her face to know all that she could have told him.

Mason knocked on the door.

Someone on the inside stirred to life. Steps sounded coming toward the door.

Mason turned to Helen Monteith. "I think," he said, "you're going to have to prepare yourself for a shock. I didn't want to tell you before, because I was afraid I might be wrong, but . . ."

The door opened. A tall man, standing very erect on the threshold, looked at them with keen gray eyes which had the unflinching steadiness of one who is accustomed to look, unafraid, on the vicissitudes of life.

Helen Monteith gave a startled scream, jumped back to collide with Mason who was standing just behind her. Mason put his arm around her waist and said, "Steady."

"George," she said, in a voice which was almost a whisper. "George!"

She reached forward then with a tentative hand to touch him, as though he had been vague and unreal and might vanish like a soap bubble into thin air at her touch.

"Why, Helen, sweetheart," he said. "Good Lord, what's the matter, you look as though you were seeing a ghost . . . why, dearest . . ."

She was in his arms, sobbing incoherently, while the older man held her tightly against him, comforting her with soothing words in her ears, tender hands patting her shoulders. "It's all right, my dearest," he said. "I wrote you a letter this afternoon. I've found just the location I want."

CHAPTER FOURTEEN

GEORGE WALLMAN sat in the creaking rocking chair in the hotel bedroom. Seated on the floor by his side, her cheeks glistening with tears of happiness, Helen Monteith clasped her arms around his knees. Perry Mason was seated astride a straight-backed, cane-bottomed chair, his elbows resting on the back; Della Street was perched on the foot of the bed.

George Wallman said in a slow drawl, "Yes, I changed my name after Fremont made such a pile of money. People were always getting us mixed up because I looked like him, and word got around that I had a brother who was a multimillionaire. I didn't like it. You see we aren't twins, but, as we got older, there was a striking family resemblance. People were always getting us mixed up.

"Wallman was my mother's maiden name. Fremont's son was named Charles Wallman Sabin, and my middle name was George, so I took the name of George Wallman.

"For quite a while Fremont thought I was crazy, and then, after he'd visited me back in Kansas, we had an opportunity for a real good talk. I guess then was when Fremont first commenced to see the light. Anyway, he suddenly realized that it was foolish to set up money as the goal of achievement in life. He'd had all he wanted years ago. If he'd lived to be a thousand he could still have eaten three meals a day.

"Well," Wallman went on, after a moment, "I guess I was a little bit foolish the other way, too, because I never paid enough attention to putting aside something that would carry me through a rainy day. . . . Anyway, after Fremont had that first visit with me, we became rather close, and when I came out here to the West, Fremont used to come and see me once in a while. Sometimes we'd go live together in a trailer; sometimes we'd stay up in his cabin. Fremont told me that he was keeping the association secret from his business associates, however, because they'd think perhaps he was a little bit cracked, if they found out about me and my philosophy of life.

"Well, that suited me all right. And then, shortly after I was married, Fremont came down to San Molinas to talk with me."

"He knew about your marriage?" Mason interrupted.

"Of course. He gave me the keys to the cabin and told me to go up there for my honeymoon. He said I could use it whenever I wanted to."

"I see," Mason said, "pardon the interruption. Go ahead."

"Well, Fremont showed up with this parrot. He'd been up to the house and picked him up, and the parrot kept saying, 'Drop that gun, Helen . . . don't shoot. . . . My God, you've shot me.' Well, that didn't sound good to me. I'm something of an expert on parrots. I gave Casanova to Fremont and I knew Casanova wouldn't say anything unless someone had been to some trouble to repeat it many times in his presence—parrots vary, you know, and I knew Casanova. So I suggested to Fremont that he was in danger. Fremont didn't feel that way about it, but after a while I convinced him. I wanted to study the parrot, trying to get a clue to the person who had been teaching him. So I got Fremont to buy another parrot and . . ."

"Then it *was* Fremont who bought the parrot?" Mason asked.

"Sure, that was Fremont."

"Go ahead," Mason said.

"Well, Fremont bought the parrot, so that no one would suspect I was studying Casanova, and I wanted a gun to give him, so I got Helen to get me a gun and some shells, and I gave that to Fremont. Then, he went on up to the cabin, and I came here to Santa Delbarra to look things over and find out about getting a place for a grocery store. I didn't read the papers, because I never bother with 'em. I read some of the monthly magazines, and quite a few biographies, and scientific books, and spend a good deal of time around the libraries."

"Well," Mason said, "I'm afraid you're going to have to readjust your philosophies of life. Under your brother's will, you've inherited quite a chunk of money."

George Wallman meditated for a while, then looked down at his wife. He patted her shoulder comfortingly, and said, "How about it, Babe, should we take enough of it to open up a little grocery store, or shall we tell 'em we don't want any?"

She laughed happily. When she tried to speak, there was a catch in her throat. "You do whatever you want to, dearest," she said. "Money doesn't buy happiness."

Mason got up, nodded to Della Street.

"You going?" Wallman asked.

Mason said, "I've done everything I can here."

Wallman got up from the chair, bent over to kiss his wife, then came over to grip Mason's hand. "I guess," he said, "from all I hear, you did a pretty good job, Mr. Mason."

"I *hope* I did," Mason told him. "and I don't mind telling you, I never had a more satisfactory case, or a more satisfactory client. Come on, Della."

They walked down the creaking staircase to the street. As Mason climbed in his car Della Street said, "Chief, I'm so happy, I'm b-b-bawling."

Mason said thoughtfully, "He does leave a clean taste in your mouth, doesn't he, Della?"

She nodded. "It must be wonderful to have happiness like that, Chief."

They drove through the moonlight, along the ribbon of road, lined with palm trees on either side. They were silent, wrapped in thought, bathed in that perfect understanding which comes to people who have no need for words.

At length Mason turned on the car radio. "Della," he said, "I don't know about you, but I'd like to find a nice waltz program somewhere . . . or perhaps the tinkle of some Hawaiian music, with . . ."

The radio screamed into violent sound in the midst of a news report. Mason heard the tail end of an announcement concerning himself, as the announcer said, ". . . Perry Mason, the noted trial attorney." There was a short pause, then the flash news reports continued, "Sheriff Barnes said merely that he had been covering dozens of places, that finding Richard Waid up at the mountain cabin which he had used as headquarters when listening in on Sabin's telephone was partly routine, partly luck. Sergeant Holcomb, of the Metropolitan police, gave a long interview to newspaper reporters. 'I knew Waid would head for that cabin,' he said. 'I can't tell you all the evidence which pointed to that conclusion, but there was enough to send me up there. Waid put up a terrific fight, but he was taken alive.' "

Mason switched the radio into silence. "We've had enough of police and murders and evidence for a while, Della. I can't get Wallman and his philosophy out of my mind. . . . I should have suspected the truth long before I did. The evidence was all there. I just didn't see it. . . . That's quite an idea, to go through life doing your best work and letting the man-made tokens of payment take care of themselves, Della."

"Yes," she said, then added after a moment, "Well, that's about what you do, anyway, Chief." She slid down on the seat so the cushion was against her neck. The reflected moonlight bathed her features with soft illumination. "Lord, think of the people who live to bless you!"

He laughed. "Let's think of moonlight instead, Della."

Her hand slid over to the steering wheel, rested on his for a moment. "Let's," she said.